I0662863

# Chocolate's
## SEVENTH DAY
# Soliloquy Vol. 3

## S. S. Suggs

## Notes by Virgie, LLC

Chocolate's Seventh Day Soliloquy

ISBN: 978-1-7369682-2-2

Cover design by: Art Painter
Printed in the United States of America

# TABLE OF CONTENT

# Dedicated...

To all my supporters, thank you will never be enough words. You believed in this story of love and passion. You made Virgie and her Noble your couple for entertainment. It is my hope that I have never disappointed you as you ventured through the days and weeks of this relationship. You made this series what is, a true soliloquy on love.

# Foreword…

Chocolate Seventh Day Soliloquy book series had me as a supporter from the first day it was published. I decided in 2019 that I would read volume one. It was after reading it that I committed to sharing this beautiful love story of Noble and his woman Virgie. I had several book parties around the city of Chicago. I invited women of many backgrounds, professions, and preferences for different book genres. We read excerpts from the book series while sharing our own experiences and emotions. We laughed, talked, and indulged. I am so excited about volume three. Volume one and two were so tantalizing, I did not want the books to end. I am here for whatever soliloquies are next for Noble and Virgie. I will continue to support the author and everything this dynamic couple has in store. If she doesn't stop, neither will I. I hope to see you at the next party!

B. Plummer, B.S.
Bachelor's in criminal justice

# Introduction...

It is the notes I keep.
They cover me.
They are like a plush blanket wrapped around me.
They clothe the four corners of what possesses me.
Circling around my mind, body, and all within me.
They beckon these emotions that enclose me.
I hear them,
I see them,
And I feel each one of them.

They shield my passion from any invasion of
distraction.
They detail my wants and desires.
They echo all of my fantasies and excitements.

Each note bounces off of the ripples of my body.
I call these notes, EUPHORIA!
I feel the intensity.
I scream from my place of elevation.
Grasping for the last touch of their melody.
Bursting to be released from my bosom.
Notes are what I want more of.
Notes are what I am in need of.
Notes are what I yearn for.
Notes are what I implore.

Noble is a strong black man who appears to have it all together. Virgie is an independent black woman who knows what she likes and needs in her life. Nevertheless, she must acknowledge that she has no idea, who is Noble Winston. The relationship between Virgie and Noble heated up in volume one. They discover what they need to keep their relationship full of passion and love. Throughout volume one Virgie learns a heart wrenching revelation about the man she has come to love.

Volume two was a journey through the layers that encompassed her man Noble. In this volume we peeled back those layers and uncover what was hidden in his heart. We discovered those things he had not shared. We discover who Virgie and Noble are both individually and as a couple.

In volume three, we continue to lose ourselves in the sensual encounters of their intimacy. But what is next for this couple? Can their loving conversation continue, or like all good things will it come to an end?

# Monday

How am I going to tell Noble what I know about Laverne? He thinks the world of her. He believes she loved him. I don't know about that. I don't have enough information about her. I would need to explain to him how different she was. I wonder if he knew. If this was something they shared or even did together. I can't get rid of this bitch Mikki. Everywhere I turn there her ass is. Now she is back in my life. I wish she would disappear forever.

Mikki should be ashamed of herself. She is always fucking up somebody's relationship. She did it with me and Kelle. She did it with D. Williams and Elynn. She even did it with her brother and his girlfriend Laurie. Now, I'm sure she fucked up Noble's relationship with Laverne. And I'm sure Noble doesn't have a clue about her, her role with Laverne, and the negative effects she has on people.

I met Mikki Jacobs at a law seminar several years back. She walked into the room, and we all took notice. She looked beautiful. Long blonde hair with big curls. Mikki is tall, skinny, and has a great body. She had on a fitted pinstripe suit with flared legs and a pair of red bottom heels. I was in awe of her confidence and fashion sense. To be perfectly honest, she is the reason I dress the way I do. Mikki sat next to me in the seminar. She was funny, engaging, and full of personality. She kept me entertained. I thought to myself that I had to make her my friend. I wanted to hang with her and help me with my style. I used to dress very conservatively for the office. I thought flashy did not equate to competence. So, I purposely dressed like I knew what I was doing. In my mind, this was the only way to dress. But the day I met Mikki all of that changed. I complimented her on her style, makeup, and confidence. She immediately told me that she sat next to me because I looked like the smartest person in the room, and she may need my help. That was far from the case. She had her stuff together. She was sharp as a sword. There wasn't a topic she didn't have insight about. And all her information seemed to be on point. I learned later that's how she gets you. She makes you think that she needs you but, you in turn start needing her.

Mikki is the master magician with her fake ass. She is fit because her ass has had a ton of plastic surgery. She appears smart because she repeats what others have said to her. She is wealthy because she has encouraged people to buy into her foolishness. She has beautiful big curls because she clips pieces of hair extensions to her hair to make it look full. This bitch will have you signing over your life savings with the lies she tells.

Noble doesn't have a clue who this bitch is and if he does, he has probably bought into her lies. He is over there sound asleep after preparing and eating a delicious meal. We ate blackened salmon, sautéed spinach, cauliflower rice, with garlic bread sticks. He even had Dutch apple pie as my dessert because he loves me. Noble had yogurt as his dessert. He eats his yogurt out of a bowl, he wouldn't dare eat it out of a container. This man and his things...

"Babe, are you okay? You are up early. I know you probably wanted some of this," rubbing his penis as he talks.

"But since our conversation was so heavy, I thought I would give you a break."

"Noble, I'm up thinking about you and Laverne."

"Why babe? Laverne is gone. You don't have to allow her to take up space in your head. What she and I had is in my past. I want to build on our future together."

"I want to tell you something, but I don't know how to share the information. I want to do it and I need you not to judge me for sharing."

"Babe, I'm probably the least judgmental person you know. You can share anything with me. That's the kind of relationship I want to have with you. Let me sit up because I want to make sure you have all my attention," as he removes the covers and places his back against the headboard.

I am so nervous but if this is going to work with us. I need to start confidently sharing what's on my mind. "Noble, you told me about Laverne and there is something I need to tell you."

"I'm listening."

I decided to sit up because this is serious.

"Noble, I used to attend swingers' parties."

"Are you serious? I would have never thought that" as he is smiling in my face like he wants me to smile.

"Yes, and why did you say that?"

"Virgie, regarding your body you are the least comfortable woman I know. When I introduced chocolate soliloquies to you, you freaked out."

"I didn't freak out. I have never been with someone who was intentional about every sexual thing we do. I'm not used to a man coming in hugging, sucking, and fondling my body before we are fucking. You named my body parts and gave each of them your undivided attention."

Noble reaches out and touches my breasts, "it's important to me to always be able to lay my head on your soft and firm pillows."

Even though this feels so good, I stop him so I can finish telling him about Mikki and Laverne.

"Stop distracting me," as I move his hand away from me.

"Ms. Lady, you are very distracting, but I will behave," as he says with that Duchenne smile, I love.

"Like I was saying, I used to attend swingers' parties with a woman who I thought was my friend. She convinced me into believing those parties would help me with my confidence about my body. The first time I went to her event I was scared to death. I was dating Kelle and felt emotionally neglected. I needed so desperately to be seen and appreciated."

"Babe, I want to hear this, but I have to be honest I am not ready to have a discussion about that dude. I am sorry but he left a sour taste in my mouth. Please don't be mad but I must be honest because you asked me not to judge you."

"Wow, Noble! I heard you out, I cried with you, I even empathized and processed your feelings with you. To say to me that you can't hear me is heart wrenching," as I say to him as I move to get out of the bed.

Noble reaches out and grabs my arm and says, "Virgie, can I admit I love you beyond words and I can't bear to hear about your love for another man. The difference between my story and yours is that Laverne isn't here but that dude is. If you can't understand that then I don't know what to say. It's my ego, my pride, my confidence, or whatever you want to call it. I looked into that man's eyes and saw the depth of his love for you. So, to ask me to sit here and hear your love for him, I can't do it. This is all I am saying."

I don't know what to say, men are different from women. I am not intimidated by any woman because I know what I possess. To hear that Noble is insecure is a little surprising. He has everything going for him and it should be obvious that I want him. I am here in this bed with him. I haven't given him any impression that I want Kelle. I just wanted to softly introduce him to the information I have about Laverne.

"Babe, can I ask you something? It's been on my mind since last week. I don't want to offend you."

"Noble, we love each other. You don't have to shy away from questions that you have on your mind. What is it?"

"Babe, I want to put my muscle in your mouth. I want you to wrap your mouth around it tightly with your red lipstick on. I want you to leave your lip print on it. I know you are a virgin speaking on the mic. I don't know how comfortable you are with doing it."

I begin by giggling and then say, "I would love too! I really liked the feel and taste of it."

Noble rolls on his back and immediately I notice I have his full attention, figuratively and literally. I get out of the bed and go into the bathroom. I apply my Ruby Woo lipstick. When I returned into the room, he was fast asleep with his dick pointed straight up in the air. This man continues to amaze me.

He is lucky I'm going into the office because I would suck him dry. Let me shut up, acting like I'm a pro at this. But I will put my lipstick on it though. His wish is my command. Natasha Janine said "Girl when you start sucking their dicks, they will be asking you to do it all the time. I see she isn't wrong either."

I used my lips to wake Noble. He was pleased. He made sure I was too, just the way I like it. Noble played with my clitoris all morning long. Now, we are leaving. Noble says he has some errands to run. I have tons of things to do today by myself.

The ride to the office is short and sweet. Noble is rubbing my leg the whole time. He says, "Babe you are so soft. I love the feel of your skin." He acts like I have never worn a skirt to work before. I love the feel of his hands, so I am in heaven. As we pull up to the door, I see Natasha Janine in the lobby. I need to talk to her. I must tell her about Mikki's ass.

"Babe what time would you like to be picked up? I should be finished with my errands by two so let me know," as he says, interrupting my thoughts.

"I will take an Uber. I'm sure I will be here all day. What are you doing that will keep you busy until 2?"

"Today is my therapy appointment. I need to contact a lawyer regarding this matter with Della. You must be in "love, love" when you start questioning me." He makes me sick with his smart ass. I was just asking. I mean I was just being inquisitive.

"For your information, I am in love with these shoes. They are the cutest pink heels I own."

"Wow, you're really doing me like this." He leans into me and kisses my lips and bites hard on my bottom lip.

"Ouch, you bit me."

"I did, I wanted to show you that those shoes can't do that. Don't love anything that can't make you feel alive."

As I walk into the building I turn to look back at Noble, he is smiling cheek to cheek probably because I gave him a tight squeeze as he was hugging me. I showed him. Don't give it out if you can't take it. Natasha waited for me in my office talking with Tabitha.

"Morning ladies!"

"Ms. Kelly, your first appointment is scheduled for 9:30," says Tabitha as she hands me a case file. Damn, that's in twenty minutes. I need to hurry so I can give Natasha this tea and go over this case file.

"Ms. Fitzgerald, can you step into my office?" I can see her rolling her eyes. She hates when I call her by her last name.

"Dang, you had to do the whole "Ms. Fitzgerald" thing. I came in peace. What have you all got up and bothered about?"

"Girl, close the door. Noble and his shit has me all riled up."

She closed the door and sat down in the chair. "What's going on?"

"Noble's ex fiancée died in his bed."

"What?"

"Yes, and he was the one who discovered it. The bad part is it happened on my birthday."

"Are you fucking serious? Does he know? This is fucked up. What are you going to do? I told you that "I never tell anyone my birthday" shit was going to backfire on you. Damn, this is crazy as hell."

"I couldn't say a word. What's crazy as hell is that she used to fuck around with Mikki's ass too. She was that lady I told you about that was so possessive of Mikki. Remember I told you Mikki said she didn't want her messing around with women at the parties."

"So, is Noble a swinger? Wow, he doesn't give off that energy at all."

"I don't know. I know one thing she was. Mikki's ass is always in some shit."

"I knew that bitch was bad news when I met her. Thank God, she showed you who she was, and you cut her ass off. You need to talk to Noble before someone else does."

"Yeah, I know."

Now I can admit I'm glad this day is over. I must call Noble to pick me up. Now that I think about it, I haven't heard anything from him. Yeah, this is strange.

"Hey Noble! How are you doing?"

"Hey babe! I'm sorry I haven't called you all day. It's been crazy. My therapist was running late. And you know how I am when my schedule is thrown off. Are you ready for me to pick you up?"

"Yes! I'm ready to go."

"Babe, I made us some dinner reservations. We need a night out. I should be there in the next 30 minutes."

"Okay, I will be down in the lobby."

"Babe stays in your office until I get closer. Remember I told you about women in heat."

"Noble, cut it out. I will be in the lobby, see you soon."

"Okay Babe, have it your way but you will get someone in trouble if I see them sniffing around."

"See you soon." Where the hell is he? Why would it take him 30 minutes to get here? This five-minute ride back to his place will be interesting. Let me wrap it up so I can prepare for his arrival.

Noble was right; it took him 30 minutes to get here. And I should have stayed in my office. I sat in this lobby with the security guard the whole time. I have no patience. If I didn't check the time on my watch every two minutes, I probably would have lost my mind.

"Hey babe, oh how I missed you. How was your day?"

"It was uneventful. How was your visit to the therapist?"

"Well since you asked, it was my last visit!"

"Why? With all that is going on, why would that be."

"It was his idea. Dr. Homon thinks I am ready to move on. He suggested that we should set up some follow up visits in the next couple of months. I want to celebrate this news."

"Noble, your therapist is not Latham Homon?"

"Yes, it is. Don't tell me you used to date him. Please I want so badly to celebrate this small accomplishment. Please babe, please don't tell me that."

"No, I never dated him. He was a named party in a civil suit brought to court. He doesn't have a clue as to what he is doing. Did you ever tell him who I was in your sessions?"

"Are you asking if I gave him your name?"

"Yes I am."

"I may have mentioned it. You know what, I'm sure I did. This is so fucked up. I paid him a fortune. What's crazy is he was ready to terminate my sessions right before we started dating then after he suggested we continue."

"That's probably why he ended them because he probably figured out, I would learn of this. I'm so sorry Noble." This man needs to be ashamed of himself. My client sued him. He took the information she shared in the sessions to seduce her and become romantically involved. Even though they were in a relationship he still charged her for his services.

Dr. Latham Homon is a charming, suave, debonair, and very handsome man. He speaks very eloquently. He uses fancy words to express himself, but they are always used in the wrong context. Dr. Homon portrays himself as well informed about mental health, but he doesn't have a clue. I'm so surprised that Noble was duped by him. I would have thought he saw straight through this fool. I guess if you are hurting and someone comes along providing you with the answers to your questions, you will believe it.

I need to find Noble a real therapist. I couldn't imagine what this fool has told him or the damage he has done.

"Babe, you don't have to worry about me. I have only seen Dr. Homon for the last two months. My previous therapist took ill and referred me to finish my sessions with him. After my initial session, he suggested that I was doing great and didn't need to follow up. So, at my next session I told him I was happily dating this beautiful woman. He then suggested we continue. I'm good, trust me. Don't worry about me. We are celebrating tonight, the chocolate soliloquies after dinner."

"Okay Mr. Noble. Let's table this discussion. I can use some Mr. Noble."

We pull into the garage. Noble is smiling so hard. He is up to something and I'm curious to know what it is. When he opens my door, he leans in and kisses me while he rubs his hand in between my legs.

"Oh how, I missed you today. I promise I will show you. I love you, Virgie. I love you so much."

"I love you too Noble and I missed you too," as I bite his lips and rub his face.

When he opens the door, I am blown away. The entire house is filled with roses, all different colors.

"Noble, oh my god! Wow, I have never experienced anything like this. How many roses are in here?"

"There are eight dozen roses in here. And another three dozen in the bedroom."

"Are you serious? You did all of this for me."

"I did all of this for us. There is no more of this me and you. It's us Babe. Us forever." I immediately started crying.

Noble walks over to me and wraps me in his arms. "Babe it only gets better from here. I need you to get it together. We have dinner reservations. I took the liberty to pick out something I would love for you to wear. Is that, ok?"

"Well, I guess I can accommodate your request."

"I need to follow up on some requests I made. Your clothing is in the bedroom."

I walk into the bedroom. There is a garment bag on the bed with a pair of some fancy heels next to it with a card. The card reads, "This note is to provide you with instructions for tonight. Please wear this garment without panties and a bra. And make sure you wear your red lips. I love Noble." So, this is what we are on. This should be fun.

I am in the shower washing and shaving for this epic night of adventures. I can hear Noble calling me from the living room. "I should be ready shortly."

I walk out in this red designer shaker dress without any underwear with my matching shoes and clutch. Noble changed his clothes while I was in the shower. He looks magnificent and smells wonderful.

"I don't know how you thought I would walk in these heels. I haven't worn heels in a minute. I hope I don't fall."

"And if you do, I will catch you. I have a car picking us up for dinner. Are you ready babe?"

"Yes, I am!"

I am having such a great time and we haven't even exited the elevator. Noble is kissing my neck when he says, "I want to taste those lips, but I don't want to mess up your lipstick. You look better than I imagined in this dress. You should wear dresses more often. Your legs look great."

As we walk out of the elevator. I see that Cheryl's boyfriend is back on the job. He waves and I wave back.

"You know him?"

"No, but I saw him last week and we talked briefly." I will not be sharing that news right now this time. We are in such a great space and that information will mess it up.

As we are riding in a beautiful black SUV. Noble is rubbing my legs and decides to make his entrance. This feels so good, but I am determined to keep my composure intact.

"Babe, how do you feel?"

"I feel wonderful. How do you feel?"

"I think this is probably a bad idea," as he continues to push in and out of my vagina

"Why do you say that?" I am trying so desperately to seem unbothered by this. He knows this is my thing and oh does it feel good.

"Because I want to make love to you right here. I told myself I would need to keep it together. I don't think I will be able to do it. Can you feel my instruments?"

"Yes, I can. But if you carry on with this pursuit I will get out of this truck with a wet spot. And I will be mortified if that happens."

"Okay, I will stop." He takes his hand out and licks the bodily fluids off his fingers. This man drives me wild.

Mr. Noble went all out. Dinner was everything. We sat in the private section of the restaurant. He took the liberty to order all my favorite foods. I want to dig in, but I was looking so good I wasn't going to mess myself up. I have no etiquette for my simple pleasure for food.

Noble wasn't on his best behavior, or should I say he was on his best behavior. He stayed in between my legs. His hands, his face, and his penis. Initially I was nervous that we would be interrupted but I learned later that he would place a flag out the curtain when he wanted the waitress to enter. This was some exclusive shit I have never been privy to. And I loved every minute of it. I even sucked his dick at the table. When I tell Natasha Janine this, she is going to die. I know she is going to be proud because my sucking game is getting better and better. Noble delights in it and it helps that I am swallowing without apprehension.

# Tuesday

After dinner, the driver drove to the lakefront, and we walked along the water. Noble made sure I had some flats. He knows how much I love walking on a hot summer night. To my surprise, we just walked. Noble didn't try anything sexual. We talked and laughed.

Noble told me that he made reservations for us to go to Florida on Thursday so I could meet his family. I am super nervous. His mother, her brother, his sister and her fiancée for a celebration. I was surprised to hear my sister MJ and Jon will be coming along with us. My sister MJ hasn't said a word. I will be calling her when I get into the office. She is supposed to give me the heads up about stuff like this. We are sisters. She doesn't let a man keep us from sharing his secrets.

"Good morning, Ms. Lady! Babe, you are up thinking early in the morning as usual," as he interrupts my thoughts.

"Yeah, you did. I had the time of my life. Thank you for everything, it was just perfect. I need to check my schedule for Thursday to make sure I'm free."

"Babe, Tabitha cleared your schedule. That's why I was talking to her. I told her to keep this week light so I could take you out of town."

"Wow, she kept that from me. I need to fire her when I go into the office today."

"Babe, if you are mad with anyone then it should be me. She didn't want to do it. She admitted that you needed the time off."

"I wouldn't fire her. I love that lady. She keeps me together. I need her."

The next thing I know, Noble is pulling me on top of him.

"Babe, can you ride my muscle like you did in the restaurant last night? You felt so good. Oh, how I love the feeling of you."

And there you have it, I rode his dick until my knees gave out which wasn't very long if you ask me. We are now dressed in the car and heading to my office.

I walked into my office and Tabitha immediately addressed me.

"Ms. Kelly, Mr. Tamor called you several times this morning. He stated that it's an urgent matter."

"He did! Well, he will have to wait. Dr. Winston informed me that you cleared my schedule for him."

"I did. I apologize if I overstepped. I witnessed how hard you work and just figured you deserve a vacation. Dr. Winston is such a great guy, and you appear to be so happy. He introduced me to Daryl. We hit it off great too. If he is half the man Dr. Winston is, I will be one lucky lady." So, Noble did connect those two. I thought that was a lie. I guess it was just a half truth.

I'm in my office returning calls and finishing up paperwork when Mr. Kelle Tamor calls back. I shouldn't answer it, but I see he's going to call until I do.

"Hello, this is Virgie Mae Kelly. How may I help you?"

"Virgie, I'm on my way to your office."

"Why would you be on your way here? You don't have an appointment and I'm quite busy."

"So, you want to have this discussion over the phone."

"Kelle, what discussion? I don't have a clue what the hell you are talking about."

"So, you are acting like you don't know what I'm talking about. Stop fucking with me."

"First of all, you called my office, and you have the damn nerve to curse at me. Get a damn life!" I hung the phone up so hard. Fuck him! Who does he think he is talking to? He better get it together. And I mean with the quickness too.

Kelle has lost his damn mind. What the hell was he thinking to call my office with this nonsense. What is his problem? He must be undone. Damn, he must really miss me or should I say miss this. Whatever it is, he needs to change his approach. This will not fly, no way, no how.

I must tell Natasha Janine about this. Let me call her.

"Hey girl, you would not believe this. Kelle's ass just called my office cursing at me. He is on his way up here!"

"Virg, you can't be serious. What the hell does he want?"

"He was talking about how he wasn't going to discuss it on the phone."

"Stop playing! What do you think it is? Do you think someone told him something and he is upset about it? First, I never even heard you say he cursed at you. You know I can't stand his ass. I'm curious to know what him has that is so upsetting."

"You know what, I never even thought about it like that. I should call him back because you're right. He never behaved like that before."

"Well, call him back and let me know when you find out something. Love you girl! I have a client waiting so let me get off this phone."

"Okay I will call you later. I wanted to tell you about what happened at dinner last night too. It's juicy too."

"I'm sure with your freaky ass," she says as she hangs up the phone laughing.

Before I could dial Kelle's number, Tabitha is calling. "Hello Tabitha."

"Ms. Kelly, Mr. Tamor is here. He said you are expecting him." I know the hell he didn't just show up.

"You can send him in. Thank you."

I stood up waiting for him to enter. I don't know what to expect. He is doing shit he has never done. I need to be on guard just in case.

Now he is walking into my office. I can see he is visibly upset. "Mr. Tamor, how can I help you?" I need to keep this professional since he wants to act like a fool. Kelle doesn't say a word. He slowly closes the door and walks toward where I stand. He is an inch away from my face.

I step back and he says while leaning into me, "I used to love you, but that shit is over, now! Why the fuck would you go to such extreme measures to embarrass me and destroy my good name?" I knew instantly, it's Mikki's ass. She told him about the video tape.

"Kelle, first get the fuck out of my face. Secondly, I don't have a clue what you are speaking of." I know but he will have to say it. I am not volunteering shit that is lawyer 101.

"Virgie, knock this shit off. Why would you fucking video tape me having relations with you then give it to a group of strangers? These motherfuckers are passing the shit around for kicks and giggles. You couldn't be that damn desperate for attention. I'm fucking mad at you. This is some despicable shit," as he turns and walks to the front of my desk.

He is totally right. This is some despicable attention seeking shit. I must own up to it. "Kelle, you are right. This is fucked up. I did what you said. I was at a low point in our relationship. I videotaped our intimate moment and shared it with a group of strangers. I never thought it would go this far."

"Virgie, you weren't thinking. Therefore, it's so hurtful. I loved you more than I loved anyone. But you violated my privacy. You destroyed my trust in you."

"I'm sure. I sincerely apologize. I thought because our faces weren't shown that no one would know who it was. But Mikki's ass had to keep telling people. People would come to the restaurant to patronize your establishment. They wanted to connect your face to your body."

Kelle interjects and says, "if this shit couldn't get any worse. So, you are telling me that people know who the fuck I am too."

"Of course, didn't she say something to you about it. Isn't this the reason you're so upset?"

"Hell no, she didn't say any shit like that to me."

"So, who told you then?"

"I saw the video." Kelle went to the swinger's event. Oh, hell no, wow!

"Your friend hosted an event at the restaurant. However, I stayed in my office. She informed me that it was a meet and greet for her social club. I heard people laughing loudly, so I walked out to see what was so funny. I looked at the screen and saw you and I fucking!"

"How did you know it was us? You couldn't see our faces."

"I know my damn body! And I know yours too! It was us!"

I am speechless. Mikki makes my ass ache! She knew exactly what she was doing. Of all the movies, that bitch purposely played the video so he would see it. I swear I should have let Natasha Janine kick her ass. Trifling bitch, I could scream.

Kelle and I were able to calmly process. He finally admitted that he understood but was still angry about it. I apologized and told him that I would talk with Mikki. I promised him that I will have her stop showcasing it and demand that it be destroyed. I think this was the part that eased his anxiety. She was supposed to do that a long time ago. I see she is not a woman of her word.

I didn't realize that Kelle was in my office for several hours. And to my surprise I haven't received a call from Noble.

I need to check on him before I get started doing something else.

"Hey baby, what are you doing?"

"Hey babe! I miss you. I was just thinking about you."

"Well, you haven't called."

"Yeah, I have been busy making reservations for our getaway. Are you ready to come home?"

"I still have work to do but I should be finishing up soon. What are we eating for dinner?"

"I know what I will be eating but I haven't thought about what you will eat," as he starts laughing loudly.

"Really Noble! You are too much. I don't have a clue what I will do with you. It is just my hope that this never becomes dull to us."

"Babe, you are stuck with this energy unless you… never mind."

"No, don't ever mind, me. Say it, unless what?"

"I don't know if I could say it without sounding rude or sexist."

"You can say it, unless what? I will tell you how it sounds, just say it."

"Unless, you desire not to have me. There I said it. This idea has come to my mind a lot. You know every day is different for us. I would love for these days to last forever. But every day is new. My only request to you is for you to keep your energy also. I want to know immediately if it changes for you. How you feel about me, the state of our relationship, your desires, needs, and the things you crave in our relationship. For my energy to remain the same I must be confident that your expectations for me are the same expectations I have for you. This sounds simple but Babe it's not."

"I am the same today as I was when we met. I'm too old to try and change it up now."

"Okay, that's what I need to hear. I have a surprise for you."

"Noble, these last couple of weeks were full of surprises. Can you just tell me? I used to love surprises, but I think I'm over it now."

30

"Ok Babe that's fair, I bought you a gift. I hope you like it but if I know you, like I think I do. You will love it."

"Aww, baby thanks so much. I should be ready around four for pick up."

"As you will have it, see you later. Babe, please know I love you so much."

"I love you too!" This man does it for me. I love to hear him say, "I love you." He sounds so sincere and heartfelt. Here he goes again taking hold of my whole attention, this man!

I picked up my cellphone to call Natasha Janine. I need to call her to tell her about Mikki, Kelle, and Noble.

"Hey girl! Are you good?"

"Hell no, this bitch Mari called and scheduled an appointment with my supervisor and I."

"Natasha Janine, you are shitting me! What the hell? Her ass is crazy! Have you told Poochie?"

"Of course, I did! He will be there."

"When is it?"

"Friday! So, I'm telling you now, I will not be taking any calls on Thursday until after this meeting. You know how I prepare for a trial. I'm going straight into trial mode for this bitch. She isn't ready but I damn well will be. What's up with you?"

"I was just speaking to Noble. He is giving me a gift that he knows I would love. You know I hate surprises. He would not share enough of the details with me. So now I will be surprised, ugh!"

"I thought you said he was very thoughtful."

"He is but with all this shit about Laverne, her sister Bella, the attorney, you, your shit, and Dominica being pregnant I don't need another surprise."

"Everything you just mentioned has nothing to do with you. Virgie, allow this man to shower you with gifts, love, and some wild sex. I know I could use a little something, something right at this moment."

"Yeah, you right. My grandmother messed me up when she told us to never take anything from a man because he will want something in return."

"You know that advice was from a different era of time for our people. But honestly, she wasn't wrong. Shit, if I give something to a man, I want something in return. The men out here now need to be needed. Hell, I need their asses, dicks, affection and their love. I know this isn't about me, but I just had to say it."

"Natasha Janine, you're right about one thing! This is not about your ass!" She kills me always talking about herself.

"Virgie, well I just had to get that off my chest. I miss the touch of a man. I like that thing I had with Mari but truthfully speaking I want to be wrapped up in a man's arms on a cold winter night. I might consider just dating women in the summer."

"You are crazy as hell. You may need to figure it out. Love has a way of changing things around. Everything you know about love has a way of making a fool out of you, right before your eyes. I used to love

Kelle. Now I can't stand his sad ass. Let me ask you this, I did play a role in Kelle's sadness. He came to my office today. After he left, I felt partially responsible for the man he is today."

"Girl, hell no! You loved that man with his simple ass. The problem I think was that he didn't know how to love you beyond your dysfunction."

"Who the hell is dysfunctional? You are crazy as hell! You can miss me with that shit. I have my shit together. It is so together that I make time to help everyone else with their shit," as I am rolling my eyes. She has me fucked up.

"That's the point I am making. You love to be the fixer. You love to come in and solve somebody else's problem. This keeps you from dealing with your own issues and problems. The first thing you discussed was how and what others are doing in their own lives. Then how it is affecting your life. You are my best friend. I have wanted you to be immensely happy. But honestly Virg, I feel like you are always on some sabotage shit. I thought you and Kelle were good together. When you started talking to Mikki's ass you began acting differently with him. Your ass loved being in that restaurant all night. I am just going to say it, you seemed the happiest during that time. I told you that bitch was bad news. Anytime you are talking to her and all she is doing is twirling her hair. She is definitely bad news. Why the fuck would she be twirling her hair while we are talking? It is because she is so disinterested in this conversation. She is fucking thinking of some other shit. And that shit has nothing to do with our conversation. She is a damn mind chaser. Chasing thoughts in her mind to fuck somebody's else shit up."

"So, I changed to Kelle after connecting with Mikki? Wow! I thought I changed him when he asked me to move in with him after he buys a house across the street from his ex-wife."

"What the hell are you talking about? What house? This is the first time I'm hearing of this. He asked you what?"

"I told you!"

"No, the hell you didn't! Do you have another best friend that I don't know about? You didn't tell me shit. Maybe it was Mikki? It had to be her because it wasn't me. Across the street from Cheryl? Wow, that's pretty fucked up!"

"And the damn house had big picture windows. We would be looking straight into each other's house. Kelle, goofy ass, thought this was the most attractive feature for the house. He was talking about it, as if he is right there watching his daughter grow up. That is when I changed. I may have told Mikki. I don't remember."

"Bye Virg, this shit has pissed me off! How the fuck are you going to share something so personal with Mikki instead of me? That's fucked up!"

Natasha Janine hung the phone up on me. She kills me with that jealous shit. It's my story to tell. I can tell whoever I want. I will call her later and apologize. She needs to cool off first.

I am standing here thinking why is Noble late. He is never late if anything he is either early or real early. I should probably call him. Maybe this is what Natasha Janine is talking about. I will just wait until he calls to say he is outside.

"Hey Babe, are you ready to be picked up?" What the hell is he talking about? Ready? I'm tired of waiting.

"Yes!"

Noble is outside waiting in his truck when I walk out of the building. As I exit the door, I don't know how he did it, but he is right here grabbing my bags. This man is a magician.

"Hello Mr. Noble!"

"Hello my dear Virgie! I have missed you so much today," as he takes me into his arms. He smells wonderful. I can stay right here in his arms forever. I'm sitting in this truck. Mr. Noble looks amazing. He has on a tailored suit with shoes on. Noble never wears shoes. He only wears sneakers, expensive sneakers but sneakers indeed. I wonder where we are going. We have passed up his condo and still driving north on the Drive. I should probably say something or at least ask where we are going. You know what, I need to sit my ass right here and enjoy the ride.

"Babe, I know you are dying to know where we are going."

"I wouldn't say dying but I'm curious."

"Yeah okay, curious, I know you. You are dying to know," as he starts smiling and waiting for me to ask.

I will not, I cannot, and I am not going to give into his idea of who I am. But he is not uttering a word. Fuck it?

"Noble, where are we going?" I have no clue why he needed to hear me ask. I can't stand him, but I love him.

"We are going to Jon's for dinner. That's the surprise I was telling you I had for you."

Why would the hell visiting Jon's ass be my surprise? "Why are we going over there? I would have at least wanted to shower and change my clothes."

"I love the smell and feel of you and this tight ass skirt," while he is squeezing my thigh.

It does feel good. I'm captivated by him rubbing these thighs. He started talking and I missed some of it.

"What do you think?"

"Noble, think about what?"

"Jon asking all of us over to his place."

"Who are all of us?"

"Well, us, MJ, your other sisters, your aunt and Raq."

"What? Are you serious? Why Raq's? And why hasn't anyone called me? Therefore, I hate surprises. What is really going on? I'm going to call all their asses and ask them what the fuck is going on."

"Babe, why can't you wait until we get there? We should be arriving in a couple of minutes."

My people aren't shit. I can't wait to see them. I think I'm more surprised that Dominica hasn't called. She can't keep a secret to save her life.

This home is beautiful. It has huge picture windows that appear to have a brown tint. There is a huge yard that is beautifully manicured. The house sits in the back of the long driveway. There is a large porch with these gigantic rocking chairs. I see there is a pool in the backyard which is as beautiful as the front. This house invites you inside. It is as if love lives here. No wonder Twaab said MJ loves his place. I understand completely. There is only one car in the driveway. I wonder where MJ's car is. I'm sure they are riding together. I know Auntie and Dominica are getting on her damn nerves. That's what her ass gets for not calling me. Auntie hates riding in a car with Dominica because she is always saying crazy shit.

"Babe, are we getting out?"

"Yeah, Noble we can get out, I would love to see what's inside."

As we walk up to the door, I notice that Noble never called Jon to let him know we are here. Maybe, he called him before he picked me up.

I love this house. I should tell Noble. This house is so beautiful. Jon lives like a family man and Noble lives like a bachelor.

Noble is just twisting the knob. These men must be close for him not to knock to enter. What if Jon and

MJ are in there getting it on? Oh Lord, I can't even believe I thought that. If she knew I was thinking that she would kill me. She is always acting like she is such a damn virgin. She hasn't always been saved and she knows I know.

"Surprise! Surprise, Babe!"

"What? Surprise what? What the hell is going on," as I look around and discover no one is even here. What the hell is going on here?

"Noble, what is the surprise?"

"I surprised you. This is your surprise! I didn't think I would be able to pull it off. I surprised you and you didn't have a clue."

A clue about what. Did he buy me a damn house? I don't need a house. He is crazy as hell. Surprise?

"Noble, can you clarify what the surprise is?"

"Okay, okay," as he grabs me around my waist and gives me one of those kisses I like.

It's intense! He is sucking my tongue, rubbing my skirt and now cradling my head in his hands.

"Babe, this is not Jon's house."

"You bought me a house?"

"Do you want me to tell you the surprise or are you going to tell me?"

"I apologize! I'm listening." It takes him too long to tell stories. I need to go to the restroom.

"Babe let's sit down. I brought you here because I wanted to playhouse with you. I have thought many times what it would be like to have a big old house.

Tuesday

The house will have to be away from the hustle, the heavy traffic and the noise of the big city. I want to watch you scurrying around the kitchen. I want to make love to you in every area of this place. Just know that when I booked it, I informed them of my intentions and they charged me extra for that," while he is laughing like everything is so funny.

"Noble, I must work tomorrow. So, you just rented this place for a night?"

"No, I rented this place for as long as it takes for me to accomplish my goals."

"Are you serious?"

"What do you think?"

"Well Noble, let's start right here!"

I jumped on his lap, and he sat there holding me. I don't know why I started crying but I just did. He didn't mumble a word.

"Noble, so I'm not going to see my family today. Is it only going to be you and me here?"

"This place has five bedrooms, four full baths, a pool, an entertainment room, a theater room, a sun porch, a guest house, a four-car garage and a 1967 vintage car. It also has a huge front and back porch as well as yards. There is a canopy, hammock, closets and cabinets. I say all of this to say, whoever you want to come here is welcome to come. But they will see, hear, and watch me make love to you."

"Noble, pinch me and tell me I'm not dreaming. I love you so much."

"Babe, I love you too. I took the liberty to have a treasure hunt created for our time here. There is treasure in every room of this house. And hopefully, you'll find all of them while we are here. I found my treasure and it's you. Virgie Mae Kelly, will you marry me?"

"Noble! Noble! what Noble?" I kissed his lips and sucked them one by one.

"Babe, I want you to be my Babe forever. Will you marry and spend life loving me so that I may spend my life loving you?

# Wednesday

What a night! Mr. Noble Winston asked for my hand in marriage. This man wants to do life with me, wow. We are about to do life together. This is a real thing. I can't help but to stare at him in admiration for the man he is, the strength he possesses, and the love he has for me. To be totally honest, I never thought marriage would be in my future.

Literally, I run when marriage becomes a thing. I prefer to take care of myself. The submissiveness part calls for another type of woman. I am not that type. I like to do what I want to do, when I want to do it, and how I like it done. I will be Mr. Winston's wife. Now, I am thinking about it. I don't even know Mr. Winston other than the fact of him being a freak, he used to be a doctor, dated Mikki's friend, and a lover who is dying to beat the hell out of Kelle's ass. I don't know this man. How am I going to marry someone I don't know? He isn't serious. Is he serious? Why me? Why now?

"Babe, you got up early doing your thinking thing. You know I'm serious about being your husband," he interjects as I'm thinking.

"Noble, are you serious? Do you really want me to be your wife? You don't even know me. Can you tell me why now? I'm just so confused. I have a million questions."

"Babe, what you need to know is that a lifetime means just that. I am willing to take this life with you one day at a time. There is so much we don't know about each other. But the beauty of it all, is there's no need to know everything right now. We can take our time peeling back the layers of our lives."

"Noble, that is why I love you. I love the man you are, the love you have for your family and friends, and your desire to love beyond what you see."

"I thought you were going to say you love the way I love you," as he squeezes my breast before he puts his mouth over my nipple.

Why can't we just talk? He always must use his power to command this body to do as he wishes. Now he is sucking my breasts with the vigor I desire. He is gripping these thighs as if he is here to collect what is due. I need to focus because he is purposefully intending to distract me. But, oh does this feel good. He knows I will stop with my inquiry as soon as he begins. Every touch from him is making my body tingle. I need to maintain my composure. I can't keep letting him do this.

"Babe, why are you tensing up? Relax! Last night, you were all in and now you are responding reluctantly. What's wrong? What's with your change in mood?"

"That's what I am trying to say to you. This is who I am. I am the type of person who allows my thoughts to push me in the opposite direction of love."

"And you are telling me this because you think I didn't know? I asked you to spend your life with me because I know that's what we both want. Virgie, you are not as complicated as you may think. You want love, to be loved, desired, and needed. Everyone wants those things and more. Fear keeps you from obtaining it. I love you and that means all of you. This is all I know and will ever know. Any information outside of that I will discover as we grow in love. So, I will ask you again but this time I don't want you to answer. You must make this choice knowing that this decision will be final. This means whatever revelation for the man I am, your past experiences, your future admirations, the people in our lives, our finances, our failures, and whatever else may hold you back. You should make this decision absent of what I or anyone thinks you should do. Virgie Mae Kelly, I want to marry you and spend the rest of my life with you. Will you grant me the honor by becoming my wife?"

I did exactly as he asked. I didn't say a word. We are lying here in the silent awkwardness of the room. The view from this room is breathtaking so I turned on my side facing the large windowpanes. I can feel Noble moving towards me, but shame will not let me face him. I am the stupidest person I know. Who wouldn't want to be the wife to Noble Winston? Yeah, I am going to discuss this later with myself when I'm not so distracted. Noble is rubbing his penis against my ass. I can feel his excitement. He doesn't play fair. He knows I have a lot on my mind. I should be lost in thought. But he wants some ass. I guess I will oblige. I start moving my ass against his penis. I can hear his delight. It does feel good. It's all strong, firm and leaky like I like it.

"Babe, I want you so bad right now. I saw you sticking your cushion out and you were ready for me to lay on them and between them. Guide me through what you want and need. My only goal right now is to please you. However, my only request is to allow me to take my time to do it."

"Noble, I have to go to work today."

"Babe, your schedule is cleared through next week. By the way, I told Tabitha she would be getting an incentive for making this happen. Allow me to please you, slowly."

I'm not saying a word. I just relish this moment. Enough stuff was said between the both of us. I want to get back to the things that bind us which are our soliloquies.

I finish rubbing my ass on his penis and he is mesmerized. I lift my right leg on top of him exposing all of me. I can feel his hand checking for my wetness.

"Babe, I need it wetter! How can I help make it wetter for you," as he then starts rubbing his fingers around.

He knows what to do and I think I'm as wet as it will get. "Baby, I'm as wet as I'm going to get."

"Babe, I want to make you squirt," as he is vigorously rubbing my clitoris.

I don't know what he is talking about, but I sure do love the feel of this. It is so intense. I want to ask him what he means by squirt. I hope he is not referring to hearing me fart during sex because that has already been accomplished. Wait a minute, oh this, what is this. Oh my, this feels so good. I feel like my vagina is tightening up.

"Babe, get ready. Get ready!"

Before I can say a word, I am pissing all over Noble. Noble is just smiling with pleasure. Now I know what he meant by squirt but how did he do it. This is my first time. Natasha Janine never told me about this. She is a total freak. I'm sure she's heard or experienced this. Her ass is holding back all the good stuff.

"Babe, how do you feel? Your release went on forever. Let's get up and take a bath."

Wow, this tub could probably fit 6 people in it. I love this house. I could live here forever. Everything about this place screams "Virgie." Noble knows me. I don't know what I was thinking. I can't believe this is really happening to me. Noble wants me to be his wife. I am really saying this, "I will be the wife to Mr. Noble!"

"Noble, can I share?"

"Sure babe, I'm all ears!"

"But I need for this conversation to be judgment free."

"I don't think I have ever passed judgment on you but if you need me to say it, then I will. I will listen to whatever you have to say without placing judgment on your decisions or choices."

"Thank you so much," as I begin to kiss him, giving him all the juices from my mouth. I must tell myself to stop before I weasel out.

"Noble, I never shared my family history, my past mistakes, and some things I have come to regret in my life. And I want to do this so that you have a true idea of who you are asking to be your wife."

"Babe, I don't need to know every detail of your life to make you, my wife."

"I know that, but I would feel a lot better knowing that you are making this lifetime commitment after knowing the good and the bad. That's exactly how I'll see it."

"Well, since you put it that way. Let me run some more hot water in this tub because we may be here for a while."

I hit his leg. Noble plays way too much as he runs the water.

"Noble, my mother died on my birthday!"

"Oh no babe, I'm so sorry!"

"I'm still dealing with it. Another sad thing about that is your Laverne died on it too. July 19 is the date I was born."

"Wow, I don't know what to say."

"I'm not asking you to say anything. I never tell anyone my birthdate because of the unresolved trauma I suffered on that day. My mother and I had such a strained relationship. I am the second oldest of my siblings and I desired for it to stay that way. She decided to have other children after me. I never forgave her for it. I was such a selfish, ungrateful, little bitch that I couldn't stand her. On July 19, 2002, I planned a big party for myself. I wanted it to be perfect. My mother told me that she wouldn't be able to come. She wasn't feeling good. But I would not take no for an answer.

I made her run errands, carry heavy items into the venue, make my favorite dish which was shrimp in a garlic sauce over linguine noodles for 100 guests and Dutch apple pie. When she walked into the banquet room, I could see that she was in pain. But I decided to ignore it and continue to set up for the party. It was about an hour later that people began bustling all around me. I discovered that my mother had passed out. The paramedics rushed her to the hospital to save her. But later that night she died. She had a heart attack on my birthday. For years I blamed myself. I knew she wasn't feeling good. I insisted on her doing everything for my party. My Auntie told me later that my mom wanted to go to the hospital to get checked out. She put off going to be there for me."

"Oh babe, I'm so sorry. This story is," as I immediately interjected.

"There is no judgment remember. Let me finish. My sister Dominica was never told this story. I had to have years of therapy to even be able to repeat it. My family decided that we wouldn't tell her the truth. She would never forgive me. My mom was the only person who understood her. Dominica lost her mind after our mother's death. We have just gotten her to start interacting with us as a family. But if she learned that it was my fault, we believe that we will lose her forever. Therefore, we keep such a close eye on her." And, just like that I start crying uncontrollably. Noble wraps me in his arms. I fell fast asleep.

I am awakened by the draining sound of the water in the tub.

"Noble, do you want to get out?"

"No babe, I will just run some more hot water. Are you finished sharing?"

"I met Laverne before."

"What?"

"Yes, I met her before. I didn't know her, but I know Mikki."

"Mikki, who is Mikki?"

"Mikki is an attorney I used to hang out with. She throws swingers parties all around the city. She introduced Laverne as her girlfriend. You sure you don't know Mikki."

"Wait a minute, are you sure it was my Laverne? Laverne wasn't bisexual."

"I'm sure it was her. I saw her several times at the events. Mikki made sure she was off limits to anyone who was interested."

Noble is now laughing loudly. I think he is laughing to keep from crying. But he won't stop.

"What is so funny?"

"Babe, you never met Laverne!"

"Don't tell me, I know for a fact I did. I can call that bitch right now and she will tell you I did." He is trying to tell me I'm wrong. He is the one who is wrong.

"Babe, you met Laverne's sister Bella."

"What the hell are you talking about? I met the lady in the picture you showed me."

"Babe, they are identical twins. Bella is the lady you are talking about. Bella is nonbinary. Laverne loved her sister but disagreed with her lifestyle."

"They are identical twins. Wow, I didn't see that coming. Can you tell them apart?"

"When we were younger, I almost slept with Bella. Laverne used to tell her all the freaky things we were doing. So, one day when I was sleeping over their house Bella crawled into the bed with me. She started kissing me all over my body. But what gave me the indication that she wasn't Laverne, was when she immediately tried to suck my dick. I knew it then. Laverne was scared to do that. We hadn't started having oral sex yet. From then on, I was able to tell them apart."

"Wow, she was trying to push up on her sister's man. No wonder why she hates you. She wants you for herself."

"Please finish sharing your story especially the part about the swinger's party. I can't believe it, uh sorry, no judgment. Tell me."

"Yes, I used to go to swingers' parties with my colleague because the bitch surely wasn't my friend. I was dating Kelle at the time when I was going to the parties. I got really bored in our relationship. He was making promises he wasn't keeping. So, I started attending Mikki's events. I never would partake in any of the activities, but I did watch. And I learned that a lot of the videos that would be played on the screens were home videos. But the sex displayed on them was terrible.

I know you don't want to hear this but I'm sharing! Kelle and I would have great sex. I asked Mikki if I could play one of our videos at the party. And she agreed. Well, the bad part is we didn't have any. I knew Kelle wouldn't agree so I secretly taped us and gave it to Mikki. Don't say a word. I can feel every ounce of your disappointment on the back of my neck. The only person who knew the video featured us was her ass. Natasha Janine never really approved of Mikki's and my relationship. She felt Mikki was a bad influence on me."

"Obviously! Sorry, go on."

"I know she was, but I liked hanging out with her. It wasn't until my birthday. I cut ties with her. Somehow, she found out when it was. She demanded that I come to a party she was having for me. I explained that I don't celebrate it. She wouldn't let up. She kept calling me. She then had the nerve to show up to my house unannounced. Well, you already know how Natasha Janine and I roll. Natasha Janine went off. As Mikki was walking back to her car. Natasha Janine started throwing rocks at her and her car. After that I cut her off completely."

"Good for you!"

"But this bitch is back to her old tricks. Kelle came to my office yesterday."

"He did what?"

"Mikki's ass told her friends that it was Kelle and I on the video. She even told them that he is a restaurant owner and where it is located. Her swinger friends started patronizing his establishment because they wanted to put a face to the body part."

"You gotta be lying. She did what?"

"Yes, she did. She went as far as to rent out his restaurant for a meet and greet. She has those kinds of events first to determine how the group will pan out for a full-blown event. Kelle stated that he was in his office and heard the people laughing hysterically. So, he walked out to see and saw us on the screen."

"Wow, they were laughing at you all. Damn, that's crazy! Laughing at my baby aww," while rubbing my cheeks.

"Stop it Noble! She was supposed to delete that video. She was not given permission to play it in his restaurant. I feel like kicking her ass. She probably had them laughing on cue so he could see it. This bitch is obsessed with me."

"So, you don't think the people just thought the video was funny? I'm sure that dude doesn't have a clue about love making."

"Why would you say that? We had great sex."

"Virgie, I doubt that seriously. You all were just going through the motions. There is no way you all were having great sex and you never had an orgasm."

"I had an orgasm before."

"The first time you orgasmed in your life was with me. I mean a true orgasm. Your first one was when I unplugged your power. Trust me I know."

Well, he isn't wrong if he is going to say it like that. My body did things that night it has never done. I have to say it is since I've been with Noble. So maybe they were laughing at Kelle's ass or my awkward ass. We will never know.

"Babe, do you feel like you are well pleased? I hope you are. If there is more for me to do to you or for you. I will!"

"Of course, I'm well pleased. I hope I never gave you any indication of me needing more. Why do you ask?" It seems I'm not the only person who needs to share.

"I'm taking you to meet my family on Friday. I'm quite nervous. You know so little about them and they know nothing about you."

I know nothing about them. To my surprise I see it is mutual.

"Noble I think you meant, "I know nothing about them" because that would be more accurate."

"Ok that's fair. Well, let's get out of this tub. I will make us some breakfast and share every detail about my family."

"But before we go, I need to slide up on this," as I slid up on top of his already erected penis.

"Oh, my muscle was bothering you. You needed to feel it. You couldn't take another minute with it on your back."

I can feel his Duchenne smile. He is right. I need to feel every part of it right here, right now.

The things this man does to this body amazes me. I'm sure it amazes him too. It is as if my body responds to his every command, his touch, and moves when he summons it. I pray we stay this way, never changing. We must stay focused on staying this way. Noble is a great man. My only fear is how he would be as a husband.

"Babe, you know I love you. And I don't mean just making love to you. We have been doing this right here for about six to seven months. You are all I desire. I want to spend every waking moment with you. When you are not here with me. I'm a total wreck. Therefore, I am so insecure about Kelle. I met this dude. If I was a woman, I would think he's a great catch. But I'm a great dude also. I often wonder if it is enough for you. Great guys don't always win. I must be honest about that. I lost Laverne! My fear is I will lose you. So, I push my overprotective piece on you. I'm telling you this because for us to work we must be transparent. I hope you noticed that I am telling the truth."

"I noticed and I understood completely. If there is anything I have learned in my years of law is that the truth is not what you can prove, it is what you believe."

"That's my exact point. For years, I thought I didn't deserve a second chance at love. Then you walked frantically into my arms. You are my everything. And therefore, I want to spend the rest of my life with you."

"Noble, are you really this guy? I guess now I need to stop being me and become," as I'm interrupted by his tongue taking my words right out of my mouth.

"I want Virgie Mae Kelly, the woman she is. You don't have to become no one other than Mrs. Virgie Mae Kelly Winston or just plain Mrs. Winston. I'm not asking you to change for me. I hope you are not asking me to change for you."

"You are correct. I want us to stay just the way we are. I love the inner you. I desire the outer you. And I will savor all of you."

"Babe, come here, that is the sweetest thing I have ever heard."

I do exactly like I'm told. I lay my head on his chest. Noble is crying. I didn't mean to make him cry but maybe he needed this release. He is always so composed. He needed to free himself. This has me knotted. I never thought I could love him more. These tears have me about to explode. I love this man so much. He is my everything. Before I finish my thoughts, this man is squeezing my ass. I don't think my legs are going to be able to withstand another go around. Oh well, the hell with it. This is what we do so let me get to doing it.

I start pinching his nipple. I take my other hand and start rubbing his strong penis. I grip it firmly then I wet my fingers so they can slide without friction. He likes this. His body is moving to my commands. Noble is still squeezing my ass. He wants me to lead. So, I will. I rub the tip of it soft then fast. I watch how his delight escapes his body. So, I rub along its path of release. Right, when I am about to take it all in my mouth. I'm interrupted by the sound of someone trying to FaceTime. I thought I turned my phone off. Who would the hell FaceTiming me?

"Babe, hold up, that's my phone." I'm saying what the fuck. Who the hell will be FaceTiming him? His phone never rings, not to mention receive a FaceTime call. We don't even do that.

Noble gets up and grabs the phone. I'm watching everything. He better not exit this room to talk either. I hear him say, "Hello mother, I'm so happy to hear from you. Are you ok? What's wrong?" I hear a soft voice respond saying, "I'm very well. I was told you will be visiting this weekend. I called to verify if this is true. Will Laverne be accompanying you on this visit?" I know she must know Laverne is deceased. Does she? This is fucked up. She doesn't have a clue about me. To make matters worse I will be her daughter in law.

"No mother! I will be bringing my fiancé whose name is Virgie. She is here right now. Would you like to greet her?"

"No Noble, that's quite alright. I will meet her when you all arrive. I can see you are shirtless and if there is a woman with you, I can just imagine it is the same for her too. Please bring some giardiniera peppers with you. Hello Ms. Virgie! And for your information, I am fully aware that Laverne is deceased. She was one of the best things in my son's life. I need you to know what my standards are. Congratulations will be held for a later date. Carry on!"

Damn, his mother is a bitch! Noble starts laughing and says, "Okay mother, I will see you soon." This shit isn't funny, not at all.

# Thursday

It's early in the morning, I discovered a note that Noble left informing me he went to run errands. Yesterday was crazy! I don't like his mother. I haven't even met her yet. She is a piece of work. I didn't even discuss that phone call with him. He didn't mention it, so I didn't say a word. I don't get involved with family matters. I will go the fuck off if someone gets involved in mine. But I will address this with him when he gets back. You know what, I am going to tell my Auntie. Let me call her now. She will advise me on how to handle his mother.

She answers on the first ring, "Hey Auntie, I have some great news."

"Virgie Mae, let me call you back. Sid and I are trying some new shit. I was trying to send your ass to voicemail. My old ass hit the wrong button," she hung up before I could respond.

Auntie knows she is a freak. It must run in our family. If it does, then MJ is one too. Who the hell am I fooling? She is not a freak.

I'm calling MJ and she isn't answering. Twaab is not answering or Dominique. I hope nothing happened. Why are they unavailable to hear my good news? Now, when they have something happening in their lives, I am all ears. Just like that I'm interrupted by Noble's calling me.

"Good morning, Babe! I know you're surprised I beat you out of bed."

"Well since you are mentioning it, I am quite surprised. What was so pressing that you got up early and left me?"

"Just running some errands before we leave tonight."

"Leave? Tonight? I need to go home and pack. I thought we were leaving tomorrow. I need to get myself together. The way your mother sounds, I need to bring my A game."

"Don't worry about her. She is trying to scare you off. Erlynn would rather I stay single so that she can control my life." Wow, his mother's name is Erlynn.

"That's the first time you have said your mother's name. I don't know any of your family member's names."

"Yeah, I don't talk about them. My sister's name is Kristin. My dad's name was Nigel Winston. My uncle's name is Connor Brooks. Babe, you will never know anyone by their names. You get to know people by their character."

"Noble, it's too early to be philosophical. I need to get myself together before I meet them."

"Babe, you said you would trust me with the details. So, I'm going to need you to do that. You will be fine. And by the way, my sister's fiancé's name is Lyon. I have hair, nail, facial and massage appointments all lined up for you. You will be perfect. Don't worry! I received referrals from everyone who

pampers you. How was he able to talk to my people?"
I told him to handle the details and he did.

"Noble, I need you right now! How much longer
are you going to be?"

"Babe, I'm on my way! I had some more stuff to
do but your needs will always come first."

"Aww, you have me right where you want me.
Take care of your stuff and hurry back."

"You sure?"

"Yes, I'm sure. I can wait but I don't know how
long I don't know long."

"Well, give me a couple of hours and I will
bring you all of me in a hurry."

I should have just told him to come home. But if
he is taking care of the details for this trip, I need him
to do that. I don't have any clothing. I should call and
tell him I'm going to take an Uber to my place. He can
pick me up there. I decided to call Natasha Janine
instead.

"Hey girl! You are not going to believe this but
Noble…" I am interrupted by her crying.

"Natasha Janine, what is wrong? Why are you
crying? What happened?"

"Girl, Poochie called me into his office
yesterday to discuss the case with these bitches. I
didn't know what to expect so I made sure I brought
my fight with me. When I arrived, he was in a meeting
with the partners of his firm that took forever so I left.
I'm an attorney too. I have shit to do. He came by my
office today. He said the claim that was brought

against me was dropped. Apparently, these bitches file claims all the time without evidence. Girl, when I tell you I was scared to death. I was scared. I owe it to your sister Dominica. I told Poochie what she said, and he was able to find a lot of shit on them. I tried to call her. I didn't get an answer. I'm sorry for interrupting you, what is it you were trying to tell me. Go ahead, I'm all ears. I just had to get that off my chest before I burst."

"I'm in shock. Dominica's ass was telling the truth about these hoes. Wow, you messed me up with this news. Wait, you said you called her, and you didn't get an answer. I called all of them. I didn't get an answer either. Let me try them again and call you back."

Something is wrong. There isn't shit I can do about it.

"Hello Auntie! I'm sorry to call you back so soon."

"Hey Virgie Mae baby, I was just about to call you. Shit, you know me, and Sid only have a couple of minutes between our old asses."

"Have you talked to my sisters? They are not answering my calls."

"I just spoke with MJ. She said she was at lunch with Doctor Jon. Hell, she is all in love. I don't blame her. If I didn't have Sid, I would have tried to get with him." She says as she bursts out laughing.

I don't know why she is laughing because there is no lie anywhere in that statement. I'm wrong because the lie is that Mr. Sid is stopping her. This is funny. I should be laughing too.

"What about Twaab and Dominica?"

"Twaab is in therapy and who knows what Dominica is doing. I'm still trying to wrap my mind around that crazy ass girl being pregnant. Every time I think about it, I start crying. What are y'all going to do? I pray that the baby doesn't get the "forget the correct shit and make up new shit" syndrome like the mama."

"Auntie there isn't anything wrong with Dominica," as she immediately interjects.

"Yes! Yes, the hell there is! I am always holding shit back from y'all. I try my best not to hurt your feelings. My sister drank during her pregnancy with that child. Dominica came in this world with that "drunken baby syndrome" shit. That's the whole reason she acts this way."

This lady is the one with the issues. Grandma always said, "Catherine doesn't have the good sense the Lord gave her." And I am not about to try to correct her.

"Auntie, I called to tell you that Noble is making me an honest woman."

"Child, so you are about to start making some money off that, huh?"

"Off of what? Did you take your medicine?"

"Child, that pussy! You've been fucking for free so long you forgot that it's a money maker. That what's wrong with y'all stupid asses. Fucking these men and barely getting a chicken wing meal. A mother fucker knows not to breathe in my direction if he hasn't brought me a fan, to wave it away. I need to start schooling y'all asses. I wish he would. You better ask Sid. His ass stays paying for shit around here. He loves every minute of it. Men were created to be the head. They are not some needy as negroes only good for fucking."

She is just going off. I can't even tell her I'm getting married. This lady just likes to hear herself speak.

"Virgie Mae, you better be listening. I'm sharing some wisdom and your ass is asleep."

"Auntie Noble asked me to marry him. I said yes!"

"Child, say that shit again! Hey! Hey! That's what I'm talking about! My baby is getting married! How many carats are in that ring? I bet it's gorgeous! I wish I could do that FaceTime shit so I can see it sparkle." Now she is about to go the fuck off. I should've called someone else. Who am I fooling? I would have had to call her anyway. I did try to call someone else. Her ass is the only one who answered. I don't have a ring! She will not process that well, so it is time to end this call.

"Auntie, let me call you back. I need to make some other calls."

"Okay, shit I need to make some calls too. My friends thought you didn't like men. I have to tell those bitches you're getting married to a man who used to be a doctor. Even though that is not anything to brag about. At least he used to have a job. Hell, Diane's son in law draws pictures of people on Madison so I know she will be excited for you." This lady hung the phone up before I could tell her not to tell anyone. Damn, I was not thinking at all. Damn,

My auntie has sucked the whole life out of my moment. You know what. Why hasn't Noble given me a ring? Maybe he wants it to be a "shared moment." He knows how much I hate surprises. He surprised me when he asked me to be his wife so he could have surprised me by giving me a ring too. I'm sure Noble is shopping for a ring right this moment, that's why he isn't here. But why hasn't he shopped for it already. If I don't like it, we can just take it back. Wait a minute is that a thing. People are out here taking rings back that they don't like. Auntie is right we need some schooling in this area.

"Babe, I'm home! Where are you?" I should answer him but since he is making me wait for a ring, he can wait for me to come out of this bathroom. I have my ass on the toilet. This toilet is just like the ones they have in Europe. It has a fan, heater, front and rear water sprayer, a pulsating function and an automatic flushing sensor. I could work from this seat forever.

"I knew you were in here sitting on that toilet. You didn't say anything when I was calling for you. What's wrong? You know whatever it is will have to wait. I need to touch you. I need to do it before we eat.

We need to get ready for our flight. I will run the shower. I don't know how long you have been sitting before I walked in here. What does it matter? It doesn't smell bad so you should be good. I want to shower with my future wife. I bought some wonderful smelling soap. I can't wait until you feel it up against your body."

"Okay, give me a few." This is some bullshit. He's been gone for hours and comes back in here with some damn soap and no ring. This is some real bullshit. I'm not thinking about his ass. Even though I could use some stress relief now. He needs to wait. I need to get my thoughts together. My materialistic ass really wants to tell him how I always wanted a five carat VVS Asher cut diamond ring from my favorite blue box store.

"Noble, I'm getting in the shower now!"

"Okay Babe, I'm on my way!"

See this the shit I'm talking about. Between him and my Auntie I should fuck myself.

"Babe, I'm ready!"

"What were you doing?" I am not for any of the silly games.

"Nothing, I took my clothes off as soon as I left you. I wanted to calm down a little because I'm frantic," looking like he just passed his final with an A.

I couldn't help but to laugh at him. However, instead of having some sensual sex we are in the shower laughing and joking with each other like nothing has me all mad and bothered.

"Babe, we really need to get moving. I can give you my muscle now or I can give it to you once we are in the car. Never mind, I will give it to you in the car.

"What? Noble, I'm going to need that now," as I point to his penis.

"I'm stressed, unsure of what to expect without my personal things, and letting you handle the details of this trip. I haven't spoken to any of my sisters about my engagement. You will have to do both. I need you!" Before I could even think about it, I'm jumping on the bed and spreading my legs wide open. He can see the path to my lungs. Look at him standing there laughing. I'm dead serious. I need to be fucked and not no damn soliloquy love making. My nerves are super bad. I need to be fucked.

"Alright Babe, but I am going to have to make this quick. I'm serious, we have a flight to catch."

"But I thought you said we are leaving tonight. There are still three hours before we reach nighttime."

"We are leaving tonight but we need to leave here to make it in time for our flight. Remember, this isn't downtown Chicago. And the car should be here in the next hour."

Yeah, he better get started because my anxiety is intensifying as he shares snippets of these details. What the hell is wrong with him? He is fucking me like a blow-up doll. "Noble, you must slow down. This right here isn't what I need. Damn, this isn't even what you need either. What's going on? You are freaking me the fuck out."

"Babe, I'm sorry! You're right! I'm nervous about the trip. I was so confident about everything. I saw you on the toilet with that angry black woman look you often have when you are not pleased. That shit fucked me up. I am sorry again. I will slow this down for both of our sakes."

"Thank you!" I'm glad I stopped him because at the rate he was going my whole vagina would have been swollen. And I wouldn't have gone on a trip with a swollen pussy.

"Babe, you are right. I cannot start something. I cannot commit to doing it all the time. I will always be slow, methodical, sensual, and passionate with you. Now come here and lay your head on my chest. I can play with your cushion first to get me back to my old self." Yes, he knows what I need. He is happy to fulfill my needs. Finally, I will be able to relax these muscles. He makes his entrance in my cushion and I can't help but to tell him how I feel.

"Yes, thank you for the way you love me. Oh, right there. Yes! That's it, yes, keep doing that," as I can feel him biting at my shoulder. He knew what I needed and thought he was not going to give it to me." Wow, was that selfish on his part or selfish on mine? I will figure it out another day.

"Yes, baby! Oh yes! I love for you to make that sucking sound. You are, oh yes, I love for you to take your time." I see Noble has learned a new trick or two. I am going to need him to get up a little earlier often. If this is the response, I get from it. This shit feels so good. I wonder if he will be changing it up in our marriage.

"Yes, I feel the wetness of me all over your muscle. Oh, I'm so wet I'm leaking like a faucet. Yes baby! Yes! Yes! Right there! Right there! I'm coming! I'm coming! Keep it right, keep it right, oh there." Wow, I really needed that release. I feel like I was packed up for weeks.

"Babe, was that what you needed? I wore myself out."

"No, I need more!" He sits up on the bed and then looks at me with this bewildered look.

"Babe, you will have to get it in the car. We must get going. Raq hooked us up on this flight. He has a friend who will fly us there. But we must be on time, or the guy will not be able to do it." I can't believe he said that Raq has friends other than him and Jon. Not to mention a friend who is a pilot. Wow, Raq must be the guy who always has a guy if you need something.

"Okay, I will get up and get dressed. It's not like I have anything to pack. This excursion didn't allow me to prepare."

"Virgie Mae Kelly, please tell me I'm not detecting you have some hurt feelings. Aww babe, you will love me for it in the end. Remember I still want you," as he puts his hand between my legs and starts fingering me.

"I thought we were in such a hurry."

"You are right! I will save it for the ride to the airport," as he looks over at me with this bright smile and then licks his fingers.

He is so nasty. I love it and wouldn't have it any other way. I wouldn't even want him to try to do it another way if he could.

This trip has stressed Noble out. He is running to the window every ten minutes. I can't wait to see what's in store.

"Babe, the car is here. Are you ready?"

"Noble, I don't have anything but my purse. How ready do I need to be?"

"Okay that's fair."

I walk outside and there is a huge car with a driver dressed like an English police officer. As I walk up to the passenger door, it opens just like an English taxicab door.

"Hello ma'am, my name is Driver. I will be the chauffeur assigned to you as you travel to and from the airport."

"I know you are the driver, but do I have to call you that?"

"Ma'am, my actual name is Driver. It confuses people all the time. I am Driver Gordon. It is my pleasure to be of service to you for your ride."

Noble walks up to Mr. Driver after he opens the door for him and says, "Thank you for helping us. I specifically requested your services. Virgie, this is Mr.

Driver Gordon. He will be," as I interject to keep him from repeating what I have already learned.

"I know he explained it to me."

"Oh, okay! We need to get going."

"Mr. Winston, do you have any luggage that needs to be put away?"

"No, what you see is what we have."

"Very good. Please feel free to activate the privacy screen once you are comfortable. Our estimated time of travel to Indiana will be one hour and forty-five minutes."

"Thank you for all you do. Babe, let's get comfortable."

This car is the size of a small house. The seats are wide and there is room for about four people. Wait one damn minute, why are we driving to Indiana? I hate that hook up shit. You must go out of your way for it. Sometimes I don't even think it's worth it. I remember traveling all over Chicago with my friend to attend events because "we were being hooked up." We had to get there early then wait to be "hooked up." This is probably why Noble is so early. This hook up is probably some bullshit with a ton of hoops to jump through.

"Noble, why are we driving to an airport in Indiana? There weren't any flights leaving from Chicago to Florida."

"Here you go trying to cross examine me to find out the details. In our marriage, I will need you to trust me. But I get it, this is our first time out of town together. You are nervous but excited. Instead of questioning me, come and sit on this muscle," as he grabs hold of his penis.

He is right about his assessment of my feelings. I should have told him in the beginning. I need to at least have some of the details he was handling for this trip. We're here now so I need to calm down. And sitting on his lap will do that.

"Babe, take your jogging pants down. I hope you did not wear any panties. If you did, then pull them down too. I'm trying to create a scene I have always had in my head. I never had sex in the back of a car. And, for us to do it in this car. I am going to erupt."

"Mr. Driver is going to kill us."

"No, he will not, it was included in the fee." We both burst out laughing.

"Did you let the privacy screen up?"

"Ma'am, I did when you were asking me questions. Now I am going to need you for this one."

I slide down onto the floor. I am parting his legs and unzipping his pants. Look at him leaning back on the couch of a car seat. He is ready to take it all in. And I am ready to do the same. I take all of it in my mouth and go to work. Even though I'm new to this, I'm quite good or maybe he is just so excited. Either way I'm doing the damn thing! We are off to the races with all this lovemaking. My Noble delivers. I take it all in with one gulp as I swallow. I let some spill out of my mouth to be nasty. I catch it before it hits the floor. I will not be the one who makes a mess on this rug.

"Noble," I yell when he scoops me up into his arms. He puts me on his lap. He is so happy to see me. I feel it in every muscle in my body. I just love this man. And, for the first time I can admit it boldly, proudly, and happily he loves me too.

He is just holding me. I thought we were about to get it on, but he hasn't made his move.

"Noble, are you good?"

"Yes Babe, I can't believe you said yes. Now, I find myself holding you. I don't want to let you go."

Before I say anything, I just kiss his neck. I lay my head on his shoulder. I am awakened by the feel of the car stopping. I look out the window. I see a private runway with a chartered plane standing by. What is happening here? Does Raq's friend have a private plane? Why couldn't we take a commercial aircraft? What the hell is wrong with me? I deserve all of this. The fact that I am sitting here questioning this is a true indication. I have unresolved traumas from my past relationships.

"Babe, you are thinking again. I can see it all over your face. Raq's friend is a pilot for a private jet company. He was leaving out tonight to pick up a client. The reason we needed to hurry is because he is on a tight schedule. We need to get off the plane before the client gets on."

"Why didn't you say that? You got me out here looking crazy. I would've spruced myself up."

71

"You would've spruced yourself up for who. You are with your future husband. I think you look stunning. What more could you have done," as he is holding me in front of him to look me straight in the eyes.

There is a crew of flight attendants and a pilot standing on the red carpet leading to the plane.

"Red carpet? Really Noble? Don't you think this is overkill."

"Babe, I'm not paying for that, so it works for me. This is how they welcome all their guests on board. It's included in the fee. But Prentice owes Raq a favor; however, I helped his mother before when she visited the emergency room. He told Raq that he would fly us out at no charge because of that. We just had to be here on time."

"Wow, thank you for rushing me. I have never been on a private plane before. And, oh how I have always wanted to."

We are walking up to the plane. Prentice greets Noble by shaking his hand.

"Prentice, this is my fiancé, Virgie. Virgie, this is Mr. Prentice Tyler. He will be our pilot this evening."

"Hello Mr. Prentice Tyler. It is my pleasure to meet you. Thank you for accompanying us tonight."

"Ms. Virgie, it is my honor! Dr. Winston took such great care of my mother before she died. I owe him more than a flight. Please join us on board and make yourselves as comfortable as possible. We are here to serve you."

Noble didn't mention that the lady died. I need more details. I feel so bad. I should extend my condolences to him and his family. Now, Noble is guiding me up the stairs like he knows what I am thinking. This man, this man, what am I going to do with him?

# Friday

Everything that happened yesterday. From the moment we stepped on that plane until now. This man is simply amazing! He loves me so much. I can't believe we are in Rome, Italy. My favorite place to visit in the world. But this time I get to share the air, this space, and this moment with the man I love. This is the best trip of my life. I will never let him go. I had no idea that we were coming here. I thought we were on our way to meet his family in Florida. Noble did say we are going to Florida, but he wanted us to come here for a couple of days first.

Tabitha is the best receptionist in the world. She gave Noble my passport. I never imagined that I would need it for this trip. Wow, God is amazing he was preparing me for something. I didn't have a clue what would happen. My workload is so heavy I never asked her about it. Tabitha had my passport this whole time. I thank God she did! If he asked me about it I would ask a million questions. He probably would have scrapped the whole surprise.

I need to stop all this stress. I need to allow someone to take care of me for a change. I will begin working on changing that. It feels good to have someone else handle the details. If he is full of surprises like these then I want more of them.

I remember when we walked on the plane. I knew something wasn't quite right. The lead flight attendant named Poly directed us to our seats. She said, "Please make yourselves comfortable," as she handed me a glass of wine and Noble a glass of champagne. I looked at her and said to myself "Florida is only four hours away. How comfortable do we need to be to fly there?" She started to show us how to work the reclining chairs. She provided us with the softest blankets and pillows ever. Poly was on it. She returned a few minutes later with a platter of sushi. It was garnished with all my favorites including soy sauce and tons of ginger.

I couldn't wait. I kissed Noble in the mouth right in front of her. I heard her chuckle because of the way he responded. I caught him off guard. I even surprised myself. When she walked away, I asked how, when and why. He said I hadn't seen anything yet.

I whispered in his ears, "I want you right here, right now."

He said, "Babe, let the plane take off first. I'm sure people have sex on here all the time. I doubt you can do it when the plane is taking off."

He was probably right. So, I sat back down.

Prentice walked out of the cockpit and introduced us to everyone on the plane. I didn't notice it at the time, but he is a very handsome older gentleman. I was listening but watching for his ring finger and his body language. Sometimes you can pick up on manners married men have. I should introduce him to Natasha Janine. Let me stop!

How would I look introducing her to Raq's friend? She messed around with Raq and those hoes. I changed my mind quick. I put my attention back on Mr. Prentice. He gave us instructions about in-flight procedures if the plane was to be involved in emergency situations. He told us to remain in our seats during take-off. He informed us if we wanted to have some "private time" to push the privacy button. The only way we would be interrupted would be in case of an emergency. Noble was right! Ha, ha, ha!

I would have to say that was my first-time making love on a plane. How exhilarating is it to do something like that? Beyond imaginable. We were flying over 30,000 feet in the air. Noble held nothing back. He feasted on every part of my body. One minute he was on the floor between my legs. Next, he was lifting my ass off the seat and sucking it. Then he was nursing on my nipples while pleasuring me with his fingers in all my holes. He had me sit on his lap. He fucked me nonstop. He even turned me over to fuck me from behind. But when he had me stand up and hold on to the chair at a 45-degree angle that was my ultimate climax. He fucked me in my ass. I became undone.

No one ever walked back into our seating area. I know they heard me. Hell, I know they heard Noble. He was saying, "I will fuck you for the rest of my life. You will be pleased with it." He was even asking questions, "Do you love my muscle in your cushion?" I played the shy girl and whispered, "Yes, Noble, yes!"

But he wasn't pleased with that answer and said, "Then shout it out!" So, I did, "I love your muscle in my ass! I love it between my legs! I love how it tastes in my mouth!" He then told me, "Stop, you are making me release. I'm not ready to do it just yet." We were fucking for so long that the pilot told us to take our seat because we were about to experience some turbulence. I know Noble heard him, but he didn't stop right away. But when we hit that first bump, we both released and then took our seats.

It wasn't until I looked at my watch. I discovered that we were in-flight for five hours. Normally, it takes forever to fly four hours. We exceeded that timeframe. I asked Noble, "Is something wrong why haven't we landed?" He said, "Because we were making love!" My nosey ass wanted to ask more questions.  I just stopped right there. After we hit several bumps in the sky, I thought I would be scared but I wasn't. I felt secure and safe with Noble. He looked nervous but he never said he was. He was acting so bravely for me. I know he was scared. The pilot then told us that we passed over the rough areas of turbulence. He took the seat belt sign off. Poly walked into our area and asked if we were ready to eat. We both were starving so Noble told her yes.

Poly returned with our first-class meal. We had shrimp cocktails, cream of broccoli soup, a gourmet salad with a raspberry vinaigrette, bread rolls with honey butter, grilled salmon, and asparagus. The food was phenomenal. We ate like we never had food before. We talked and laughed. We were exhausted but I wanted to suck his dick so bad. I was determined to have some energy to do it before we exited this plane. I kept telling myself I needed to hurry up and do it before we landed.

Poly returned to retrieve our plates. When she exited the room, I began rubbing in between his legs. He didn't resist. I leaned over to kiss his chest. He loves that. I put my tongue on his nipples which drives him crazy. I slid onto the floor in between his legs. I first started rubbing his dick up and down. I was sucking each one of his nipples. And he moaned and groaned with delight. So, I took my tongue and trailed down his chest making circular motions. He grabbed my head and started massaging the back of my neck.

When I told you it felt so good that I stuck my own fingers in my vagina for pleasure. I took his dick in my mouth. I started sucking away while I was masturbating. I went to town. I realized I didn't put the do not disturb button back on. Poly walked back into the room. Normally I would have been totally embarrassed but I wasn't. This is my forever dick. I will suck it when, where, and how I want. She acted as if she didn't see me. I heard her ask Noble something. I heard him say, "give us a few minutes," between his moans and groans. I sucked it until he came. This time I held his semen in my mouth and kissed him with it and he received it all.

Next thing I know is, Noble is telling me we needed to clean up because we will be landing soon. I went to the restroom to clean myself up. When I returned to the seat, I felt like Poly was giving me the thumbs up approval. We made eye contact as she was cleaning up the seating area. I just smiled back at her like "you better recognize."

We were sitting in our seats and Noble leaned over to me and said, "I'm so proud to make you, my wife. I love you forever. Thank you for allowing me to handle the details. You will not be disappointed."

The next voice I heard was Prentice saying, "Thank you for trusting me to fly you all to Italy. Welcome to Roma, Italy! We enjoyed having you on flight Love Forever as our passengers!" I turned to Noble and immediately started crying. He took me to my second most favorite place in the world. The first is being in his arms.

The surprise didn't stop there. When we exited the plane, there was a driver waiting for us. It wasn't the car that drove us to the airport in Chicago but nevertheless it was a nice spacious vehicle. The driver only spoke Italian. I looked at Noble. I was saying to myself how the hell are we going to communicate with him. When Noble started talking to him in his language. I didn't know he spoke Italian. He is forever amazing to me. Noble said he was asking if we wanted to stop somewhere else before heading to the hotel. He also said he told him that we just wanted to go to the hotel. We wanted to finish making love. I was so embarrassed, but he wasn't lying. I saw the man smile and off we went.

79

# Friday

We are staying at this beautiful hotel in a suite large enough for a family of ten. It has every amenity known to man. There is a king size bed, 70-inch screen television, a plush convertible couch, large tub in the middle of the bathroom floor, and my favorite "bidet" with all the bells and whistles. Noble told me after we entered the room, "We will utilize every area of the room before we leave for Florida." That is no surprise. He was acting like I didn't know that already. Those were my same sentiments.

"Good morning, Babe! How are you feeling?"

"I am feeling wonderful! I don't know if I will ever come off this cloud. Thank you for this. Thank you so much. You listened. You paid close attention. You handled the details. I'm so happy!"

"Babe, what else was I supposed to do? I listen to you through your messages verbally, non-verbally, and your written requests. You bring me so much joy. I count it as an honor to handle what it is you need and desire. Today, I have some exciting things planned. But first I just want to lay here holding you. Then we can get our day started." I even felt a few tears rolling off his face onto my back. I didn't say a word. There is nothing to say he poured out his heart. So, I laid here receiving every bit of it.

As we were getting out of bed, I was reminded that I don't have anything to wear.

"Noble, we need to go shopping. I don't have anything to wear."

"Babe, remember I handled the details. We have everything we need. It was at the house with us. It traveled with us. It is inside of the closet."

I'm running to the closet to see for myself. There inside I find four designer suitcases. Two suitcases with my name on it and two with Noble's name on it. I don't even wait for his permission to open them. I lay the large suitcase on the floor and open it. I am speechless! Noble has the most beautiful sundresses packed in it. I have some sexy panties and matching bras. He knows how I love for my underwear to coordinate with my outfits. There is a hygiene kit. My makeup bag is filled with new makeup items. He even bought me some new oils and lotions I love. I open the small suitcase. I discovered that I have two pairs of designer sandals, a pair of designer sneakers, and some plush socks to wear to bed. There is a note that says, "I prefer your skin touching mine, but I know you rather have clothing. Love Noble."

I get up off the floor and jump on top of him. What did I do so well that he became the man for me?

"I guess I did a great job."

"You did a magnificent job. I was worried. You couldn't have accomplished this in just a couple of days."

"To be honest I have been working on this for a couple of weeks. Tabitha was great. She assisted me when I had doubts or questions."

"Wow, I'm so impressed. No one has ever taken the time out to pay attention to me. Thank you for loving me enough to want to take care of me."

"For you, anything and I mean it."

"I wish we could lie in this bed all day. I have more surprises. If we don't get going, we will miss all the other epic adventures this day holds for us."

"I would rather stay right here, with you, every way you will have me."

"Babe do not do this to me. Please allow me to do this for you. Can we get dressed and embark upon everything this city has to offer? Please! I promise tonight I will give everything you need from any of my muscles."

"Okay, I will not tempt you into staying in this bed with me." Oh, how I want to. I can fuck this man every day. All day, if it was up to me. But we are in the city of love. I want to experience love with him.

We are dressed and walking out of the hotel. I feel like Vivian holding on to the hand of my man. Noble reserved a car to take us around the city. When I say I'm in heaven, it's a mere understatement. He looks so handsome and sexy. His confidence is breathtaking. For the first time, I can truly say I'm happy. Not one time, have I even thought about checking in with my family and friends. I am fully vested in this moment. Noble has my full attention. We shopped, dined, walked, talked and laughed. This has been truly a much-needed vacation from everything that distracted us from being us.

"Babe, we will head back to the room for a quickie. We need to change for dinner. I picked the perfect dress for you to wear. I hope it is acceptable to you."

"A quickie? Roma has you in the quickie mood. I thought you like the passion that comes with our soliloquies."

"Babe, I do! But being here with you right now is driving me wild. I will take it anyway I get it so that we are not late for my surprise."

"More surprises? Wow, when will it stop?"

"It is my desire for them to never stop," as he gives me one of those wet juicy kisses. I can't wait to get back to the hotel.

As we enter the room, I notice that there are two garment bags on the bed. I walk towards the bed when he grabs me and wraps me in his arms.

"Remember quickie first!" Noble slides my dress up over my thighs, he inserts his fingers inside of me making me gasp for air. I needed this so badly. I needed to become unplugged. He turns me around. I slightly lost my balance.

"Babe don't fall on me. Let's move to the couch. Grab hold and let me do the rest." He didn't have to tell me twice. I am doing just that. I walk over to the couch, but I am taking my dress off. A quickie is good, but he will have to do it while I'm butt naked.

"Babe, hold on and don't let go."

I'm closing my eyes. I want to take it all in. Noble is grabbing my waist. I feel the total force of his entrance. My legs start to shiver. He keeps going and going.

"Oh baby, you act like you missed me," as I say before he smacks my ass.

"Was I a bad girl? Or is this smack for being a good girl?"

"This is for being my girl," as he smacks my ass a second time. This time it stings a little, so I yell, "Ouch!"

"Now you get to see the rough side of me. Can you handle it? Can you handle this," as he smacks my ass again?

"Yes, as long as I can have both sides of you."

"Yes! Yes! Yes, you can have all of me! Any way you want it." And we release together.

Noble picked out a strapless tulle mini dress with a pair of crystal heels. I always knew he had great taste. This is the next level. I would have never opted for a dress like this. He is wearing a tan linen suit with a Pima cotton shirt with a pair of brown leather Italian shoes. We look damn good together.

"Baby let's take a picture. I want a memory of this moment." I pull out my phone. We stand in front of the mirror and capture a picture for the world to see in the future.

When we get downstairs, the car isn't there. Noble pulls out his phone to check it. I am just standing there when a white carriage pulls up.

"Babe, here is our ride." He's got to be lying. We are going to dinner in a carriage. I just died.

"Have you ever been inside one of these?" I have! I am not stealing his moment.

"I have never ridden in a carriage to dinner." There was no lie in that statement.

"Let me help you up. Hold on to my hand."

If I had on panties, I probably would have peed on myself. I leaned my head on his shoulder and before I knew it, I'm crying.

"Hey! Babe, no crying even if the tears are happy tears. There is so much more I have planned. I want your face as it is now."

"Really Noble, let me be!"

"Okay, just a couple more tears then."

We pull up to a restaurant that Natasha Janine and I visited when we traveled to Italy. This bitch is in on this too. Wait until I talk to her. She could have given me a heads up. To be honest I am glad she didn't.

"I have eaten here before."

"Are you serious?" He says with a smile on his face.

"Yes, I am serious!" He leans in and kisses me.

"This trip is all about you! Counsel, I thought you would have figured that out by now."

"Well, if you wouldn't keep distracting me with all this sex. Maybe, I would have. You don't play fair; I see that now."

"I thought I was playing just like you like it."

The restaurant is a small quaint establishment run by a traditional Italian family. Natasha Janine and I stumbled on it as we were walking along the road to the Colosseum. The food here is very good with a rich flavor. There is an older man who sits outside of the restaurant. I think he is the owner. It is managed by an older woman and her three sons. It sits at the bottom of a hill. Tonight, it is filled with people. There is live music being played and everyone is dressed up. The energy here is high. I always said if I ever were to come back to Rome. I would eat here again. And only Natasha Janine's ass knew that. She got me with this one.

We are sitting in the middle of the restaurant enjoying our meal. When the waiter walks over and whispers something in Noble's ear. The next thing I know is the music stops. Noble gets out of his chair and walks over to my chair. He asks me to dance. I stand up and take his hands. We are slow dancing in the middle of the restaurant. The band is playing "So Amazing" by Luther Vandross which is my favorite song. Now I'm crying all over again. I'm trying to hold it in, but I can't. He will just have to deal with my crying face.

We are walking back to the table. When I noticed our plates were removed. Noble pulls out my chair and kneels next to me on one knee.

"Virgie Mae Kelly, I asked you before we traveled here would you be my wife. Your answer was yes! My prayer is that it is still yes!"

"It is still yes!"

"And it is because you said yes. I present you with this ring." Noble pulls out from his pocket a little blue box with a navy-blue bow.

"We are in your favorite vacation spot, in your favorite restaurant, dancing to your favorite song and your dream engagement ring. I commit to wed my favorite woman on earth."

I can't recover. I cannot recover! I am shaking right now! I lost all my composure.

He can't be serious. How? When? I'm going to kill Natasha Janine! She told him everything. Oh Lord, did she tell him everything? Oh my God! Everything I asked for, desire to have, the place I wanted it done, and to have the perfect man to do it. I must pinch myself to make sure I'm not dreaming. This man loves me beyond what I envisioned for myself to be loved like. How? Noble? Wow! This can't be real.

"Babe, will you take this ring?"

I am so consumed with my thoughts that I never extended my hand.

"Yes! Noble, I love you so much!" I reach for his face after he places my engagement ring on my left ring finger.

"Babe, you scared me. Thank you for accepting this small token of my love." Wait, it's not the three C's I requested. I didn't even look. Woo, it is! I thought he bamboozled me. He plays way too much.

Now, I can't take my eyes off it. Hell, I forgot to get my nails done. My hands look terrible. Why does he have me out here looking goofy with this stunning ring on my finger? To be honest I have never tried my actual dream ring on my finger. I designed it in my head, but I'm amazed at its brilliance.

"Babe, we have his and hers spa day tomorrow. So don't start stressing about how your hands and feet look. We fly out tomorrow night for Florida. I will introduce you to my family as my future wife. It was very important to me that you had time to relax, release, and cry. I know how sensitive you are. I do not want you stressing yourself out about what's next. You love me?" He asked me while staring in my face. I love looking into his beautiful brown eyes.

"I love you more than I loved anyone." He makes me happy.

# Saturday

After last night, I am so excited to love someone. Noble is my first true love. The love of my life and my forever. It is not because of all these things he has done for me. It is because of how he loves me. His love is soft, tender, passionate, embracing, strong, safe, kind, mesmerizing, and mysterious. He is a giver, sweet, thoughtful, nurturing, and romantic.

Noble makes it easy to love him. This is the thing. Love should be easy but not without sacrifices. I think people have a misunderstanding when they are seeking love. Some people believe to love another person is to sacrifice yourself in the process. Sacrifices are the same things as challenges. They are the things people are willing to remove for the betterment of the relationship. Be willing to pursue your own desires. You must be willing to give what you have if it can make the relationship better. Noble does that for me.

I'm willing to give up on those things that hold me back from his love. The one that comes to my mind is my need to control everything around me. I never really paid close attention to it. My friends and family all made mention of it. I disregard it. I believe that if I can't do it then it can't be accomplished. To relinquish control, means I am allowing myself to be vulnerable.

Vulnerable is a word that scares me. To me it means that my emotional walls can be damaged at any moment. Love requires people to be vulnerable. It expects you to love differently. And what I mean by that is with every relationship I must be open to someone new. I feel vulnerable with Noble. I love and trust him. There is still something mysterious about him and his family. Is he vulnerable with me? Has he let his walls come tumbling down? I feel there is still something he is holding back from me. And for this engagement and marriage to work then I will have to see his vulnerability.

"Babe, I'm laying here watching you while you are intensely thinking. Did I do something? Are you okay? I feel like every time I have conquered a milestone with you. I may not have done enough. Tell me why you are so reluctant to receive my love for the world to see."

"What does that mean?"

"It means allowing me to love you without stipulations. To love you without parameters. It is without expectations. It goes beyond traditional methodology. It is the kind of love you have without the opinions of others. My goal as your husband is to love, protect, support, encourage, provide and to fuck you forever. I apologize for my language but that's exactly what I will do. You will be warm in my bath. I will be the basin that holds you in."

"You are too funny. And not to mention you sound like an old man. When you use a word like "fuck." I hope I don't disappoint you. My examples of being a wife were far from exemplary. I don't know how to do it. I fear that I will not be able to do it correctly."

"Babe, I don't know how to be a husband. But I know how to love a woman. I will start there."

"Noble, will that be enough. We have been dating for such a short time and are now getting married. I want nothing more than to be your wife. I must address the elephant in the room. Are we moving too fast?"

"Yes, we are. Life is too short for us to take our time. We love each other! We desire each other. Why should we wait? Wait for what? I want what we have now. We are too old to be in a dating relationship. We both loved people before and lost. Why not try to work on loving each other forever? We can figure out the small stuff later like where we will live, how many cars we need, whether we will have children or not, how bad is our credit together or separate. I want you two trust me. I promise to be a man that listens, compromise, and lead while supporting you. I love you!" This man melts my heart away.

After our good morning sex, we are in the car heading to the spa. Noble is right. I do not need to try to figure this one out. I need to just let it be. I will take a chance here. He is a great man and that's more than enough for me. "Babe, I booked the spa. I left it open as to who will service us. Do you prefer a male or female?" This is a trick question. I think I will fail. I will try.

"I would prefer a male." Please don't get all sensitive and overprotective about my body.

"That's fine, I prefer a woman myself. Is it okay for a woman to massage my muscles?" He is sitting here flexing his muscles in my face.

"It's okay with me as long as she doesn't flex this muscle," as I grab hold of his penis.

"Gentle there, young lioness. This man has been working overtime. He is a little weak," as he places his hand over mine. We both start laughing. He is completely right. My girl is a little ginger herself.

The spa was amazing! Noble is so bogus for reserving an older man and woman for the massages. When I walked into the room, I observed several athletic men and women scurrying around. I just knew we would get a pair of young, sexy, and eager masseuses. We were sitting in the room when this older man, probably in his early 50's walked into the room then later accompanied by a woman of the same age. I looked at him and said, "I see you have a sense of humor."

He looked at me and said, "No God does! I asked for an island girl with a perky bosom." I hit him so hard. I wish he would have tried it too. He just laughed and wouldn't stop laughing. I didn't think it was funny. I laughed too to play it off. He would have learned quickly. I don't play about my man.

This trip is one for our history books. We are flying back to the states but this time on a commercial plane sitting in business class. I asked Noble why we couldn't sit in first class. He said that he didn't want to be apart from me. I think it is because he wants his hand to stay between my legs just like it is right now. He is so nasty with his freaky ass.

"What should I expect when I meet your mother? She wasn't the sweetest when she called the other day."

"My mother is harmless. She is all bark and no bite. You are the second person in my life after Laverne. So, she is quite unsure of who you are. Be yourself! I promise she will love you."

"Did she like Laverne?"

"My mother and Laverne had a strange relationship. They both wanted to be the center of my attention. They found it difficult to share me. I did what I could to show them that there was no need for that. My mother thought Laverne was too controlling. She believed I may have gone further, in life, if I was not with Laverne."

"Why did she feel that way?"

"I always wanted to be a plastic surgeon. My father was a plastic surgeon. He would tell me all the things he was able to accomplish in surgery. I was always fascinated by it. So, when I went off to medical school, I told Laverne what I wanted to do. She would constantly remind me of how my father was with my mother. And she begged me not to do that with her."

"How was your father with your mother?"

"He was insensitive and cruel. He worked long hours. He would often leave her to take care of two children on her own. I would assure Laverne that I was nothing like him. She could not see past my mother's reality. My mother knew that Laverne didn't want me to be a plastic surgeon. She knew Laverne was passing judgment on her."

"Laverne sounds like she was controlling."

"She was controlling. I loved it. It allowed me to have someone who loved to take care of me. As a young man trying to find my way, I can admit I needed some help. She was my everything. Laverne helped me to discover the love I need in my life. Babe, you know you are controlling too."

"No, I am not. I'm not controlling. I let people do them."

"Yeah okay. I like what I like. You're the controlling woman I like," as he kisses me in my mouth while pinching me on my labia.

"Were your parents married when your dad died?"

"Yes, they were. They were married for 35 years. My mother was unhappy for 32 of those years."

"What?"

"My mother married him because she loved him. He married her for her money. My grandparents were hard working people. My grandfather was a self-trained gardener. He worked for a golf course. His job responsibilities were to keep the grass green. My grandmother worked in the kitchen of the golf course. She was responsible for making sure the food was always delicious. They came from nothing. They decided they would use the information from the patrons to become something. They invested when people were talking about investments. They sold stocks when people would talk about selling. They did everything they heard the patrons talk about doing. They would smile the whole time like they didn't understand. This made people feel like they could continue talking comfortably in their presence. They had a plan. They executed it. It made them very wealthy, but they didn't stop working. They worked until their health failed them. So, my mother and her brother never had to work. My father met a young lady who had more than she needed. He used that to further his aspirations of becoming a doctor, father, and terrible spouse. The first time I heard him tell my mother he loved her was when he was on his deathbed. She cried for days because she never thought he would ever say those words to her."

"How was he as a father?"

"He was great! We loved and adored him as our father. He just was not a good husband. Laverne always feared I would become him. And my mother feared that Laverne would become her."

"What do you mean?"

"My mother said that I never loved Laverne. She believed I loved the things Laverne did for me."

"Well now that you had time to seek clarity, did you?"

"Did I love her?"

"Yes Noble. Did you love Laverne?"

"I loved what she did for me. You are my first true love! Laverne was the first woman I knew

95

intimately, passionately, and emotionally. When she died, I thought I was lost with despair? But my soul-searching travels showed me that I was relieved. I didn't have to leave her because she left me.

As a young man, I was so intrigued by the things she taught me. It was the things we would do and the places we will go. She was too controlling. She was suffocating me. When I achieved what she wanted, she would distract me from moving further. So, after I discovered what my mother had been telling me my whole life. I called her and admitted she was right. My mother thinks you are using me." What the fuck is she talking about me?

"Excuse me!"

"She thinks that you are using me because I am a doctor."

"You gotta be lying. I'm using you? Did you tell her I'm a successful lawyer who has her own money?"

"No, I didn't."

"Well why the fuck wouldn't you tell her that. I'm not a gold digger. I don't need a man for nothing. I really mean nothing. I can fuck myself good. I have done it for years."

"Babe, calm down. She still thinks I'm a doctor. She has dementia. It's not an attack on you. She is stuck in a period that does not allow her to distinguish between the past and present." Wow, I forgot. I was about to go to hell off. Damn, I'm glad he cleared that up.

"My mother is a true sweetie. She is a well-manicured woman. She is the most popular person in her community. My uncle Connor is her only sibling. He adores her. He sees it as an honor to care for her. Connor is a rich man who is free to be free. There is only one rule he must follow while taking care of my mother. No man or woman is to reside or stay the night in her house. She is very accepting of his lifestyle. He is respectful of her wishes."

"Your uncle Connor is gay?"

"He is nonbinary." Wow, there is a lot of stuff going on in this family.

"If your mother has dementia, then how am I to develop a relationship with her as her daughter in law. She will never accept me or get to know me."

"That's a great question. I don't know. I do know this. I am madly in love with you. I don't want to go through life without you. This is what takes precedence in my life. I will deal with the other stuff when I must."

Talk about a bomb shell of information overload. His mother has dementia. She doesn't know he is not practicing currently. Does she even know that Laverne is dead? What about his sister and her fiancé?

"Noble, if she thinks you are still a doctor. What about Kristin? What does she believe in?"

"She believes Kristin is a teenager and that she lives with me and Laverne. We never tried to clarify the details for her. What she thinks won't hurt anyone? I mean until now. We must clear it all up so those who love us are not hurt by it." Wow, this is a lot. A whole lot that I am discovering in the final hours leading up to the meet and greet.

For the first time, I'm not in the mood for any of this playing with my cat. He has dropped this bomb shell on me. And I'm supposed to go back to business as usual. I will not, I cannot. His mother is sick and not only sick but can't remember. His uncle is an unemployed, non-binary man and spoiled rotten to the core. Connor cares for his sister. He is trapped within the house. Noble's sister is another spoiled rotten woman. She has the support of her family. She is marrying a man they don't even know. Just like me. What the fuck am I entangled in? This shit must be a joke. This can't be real.

"Babe, there you go again."

"What? There I go again? What the fuck is that supposed to mean?"

"Hold up! Why are you speaking to me like that? Don't talk to me like that."

"Talk to you like what."

"With that tone! The tone you are using. I don't deserve that."

"Well, I apologize."

"You know, this isn't the place. If this is your apology, then miss me with it."

"Noble, what's wrong with you? I said I apologize."

"Exactly you said it." Now he is sitting here mad. Shit, I know I shouldn't be mad but for some reason I am. All this shit is fucked up. Fuck it! We can fly back to the states in peace and quiet for all I care. I need the time to think anyway. Hell, I didn't sign up to be a part of this circus. I just wanted a man who loves and adores me. I wanted someone to take care of the details. I wanted someone to understand me and what makes me tick. I wanted some uninhibited sex and some unconventional love making. I wanted a man who was tall, handsome, had his own money, and loved to have a great time. I wanted a man who would walk through walls for me, with me and after me. I wanted a man like Noble. Damn, I am always sabotaging shit. What the hell am I doing?

"Noble." I say it with the sweetest voice I can muster up.

"Yes?"

I lean into him to whisper in his ear, "Forgive me! Not because I'm asking you but because you want to, please." Look at him taking a deep breath.

"I forgive you because I love you. I know I shared a lot in a matter of minutes but at a least I shared."

"I know. It was a lot and allowed me the time to process it."

"I never rushed you into processing it. It can be years before you take it all in. I want you to be my wife not for my family's sake but for mine. I do not want to do the rest of this life without you by my side."

That's probably the last thing I remembered happening before I was awakened by the announcement of us landing from the pilot. I look at Noble and take a deep breath. Whatever I journey upon with the Winston's, I'm doing it with Noble. I should be okay.

We were at baggage claim retrieving our luggage when I heard a woman calling, "Nob! Nob!" It doesn't take rocket science to know they are calling Noble.

"Noble, do you hear the lady calling you?"

"What lady?"

"The lady over there. She keeps saying, "Nob! Nob!"

"Babe, that's not my name," he started laughing hysterically.

"I would have thought Nob is short for Noble."

"Why would anyone need to shorten the name Noble? It's only five letters."

"Well, I guess you are right. Who is picking us up from the airport?"

"We are taking an Uber."

"I guess all of those surprises have me curious or on edge or even suspicious."

"Oh okay! You can snap out of it. Surprises are all over for now." He makes me sick with his smart ass.

This ride is taking forever. I feel like we've been in this car longer than when we flew from Italy. I think I may be anxious about what or who awaits me. I have so many questions but after my episode on the plane I need to keep my damn mouth closed. Noble hasn't really recovered from that. He has been quite the quiet mouse. Even his hand feels different but knowing me it may all be in my head. No, it isn't. He is not even responding to me rubbing his hand. Normally, he would rub my hand with his thumb and index finger back. It is stiff and lifeless. Good job Virgie, you can fuck up something in zero to thirty seconds flat.

Finally, we arrived. We are pulling up to a large gate that reads, "The Winston Place." They have a damn estate! He didn't say that. If my nerves weren't already on edge, I'm about to pass out now. He is a modest mother fucker. He didn't mention shit about "The Winston Place."

How the hell am I to act now? This man, this man is trying to send me to an early grave with these damn surprises.

When Uber stops at the gate, we hear a voice saying from the audio box at the gate, "Welcome home Mr. Noble. Raq is headed to the gate to meet you." Why the hell is Raq here? What the fuck is going on?

"Why is Raq here? Does he live here too?" Now he is just sitting here like I'm not asking questions.

"Noble, do you hear me? Why is Raq here? What is going on?" He still didn't answer. This is stupid as hell. He is so mad that he can't answer.

"My mother does not like people driving on her land that she does not know. We will get out at the

101

gate and Raq will drive us up to the house." This bitch is crazy for real. The cab can't come on her property. Wow!

"But why is Raq here? Why does he have to come and get us?"

"He is in town and is staying here with us. Norman would normally come and pick us up, but he is seeing to the guests."

"You are referring to your sister and her fiancé as guests. That's strange."

Rich people have it bad. They are so impersonal with each other. My family and I would never consider ourselves as guests to each other. Shit, their houses are my houses. My house, well it's my house. But they are not guests of it, they are my family.

"Hello Mr. and Future Mrs. Winston, welcome to The Winston Place."

Noble over here doing the chest bump shit with this damn clown. I can't stand Raq's ass. I hope he sees it all over my face. I don't care if he did get me a free plane ride to Italy. Fuck you, Chump!

"Hey Raq!" And that's all he is getting.

"Virgie, I see you are still colorful with words."

"Yeah whatever!" Noble is giving me a disapproving look. I don't care. He should have expected that. He knows how I feel about him.

I tuned out. Noble is catching him up on everything. He is talking to him like some school age boys reminiscing about their encounters. I'm surprised Noble is even sharing it with him. I would have thought he would be closer to Jon then this clown. Jon is the more normal of the two.

He pulls up to the entrance of the house. A man is standing in the doorway. He must be Norman who Noble was talking about. Raq exits the car and says, "Dad, there are a total of four suitcases and two garment bags."

"Okay son! I will have them brought in the house and up to the room."

Norman is Raq's father who works for Noble's family. Get the hell out of here. What just happened? I missed something. Raq's father works for Noble's family. Hell No! This is crazy as hell. This would explain why they were friends and why they are so close. Wow!

"Hello Ms. Virgie! I have heard so many wonderful things about you." About me? I haven't heard a damn thing about him.

"My name is Norman Winston. I am Noble's uncle." I'm shocked. Noble's uncle? This is his father's brother. What is happening here? So Raq is related to him. Wow! I'm totally speechless.

"I know you know my son Raq."

"Hello Sir! It's a pleasure to meet you. I am very familiar with Raq." I should tell him about how he almost fucked up my friend's life with his bullshit. Noble would kill me so let me keep my mouth closed.

"Hello Nephew! It's been a long time. Oh, how I missed you! I'm so sorry, congratulations are in order. Ms. Virgie, thanks for making him an honest man again. I wish this one right here," pointing to Raq. "Would find a nice woman and sit his ass down. Pardon my colorful language."

I like this man already. He is right about all of it. Noble gives him a big hug. I can tell from the embrace that they are very close.

"Hey Unc, I missed you too. Thanks for being here."

"There's no other place in the world I would be."

Norman leads us through this large foyer. He turns to us and says, "Everyone is in the garden."

Oh, these are the guests Noble mentioned. Why the hell does it need to be a celebration? I guess because the prodigal son returned home. If it was me, I would be here taking care of my mother. They are celebrating him like he is somebody. He hasn't visited in I don't know how long. When Norman opens the doors. I began to stumble. Noble catches me and says, "Surprise!"

My whole family is here plus Mr. Sid.

"Babe, surprise! Surprise! Are you surprised?"

I can't stop crying. He flew my whole family out here.

"Sister, I heard that you said yes!"

"Dominica, oh my God! How? When? Oh my God! I tried calling you but none of you would answer."

"Noble threatened me. He said if I said a word to you, he would kill me. Sister that scared me. I gave my phone to Twaab. I can't die with a baby in my stomach. He would have killed two people. Then, you wouldn't ever get married because of how bad this turned out." Now I'm crying and laughing.

"Auntie, you knew of this and didn't tell me."

"I sure didn't. I wasn't messing up my free vacation with rich folks. That's why I hung up on you. Your nosey ass just had to call me back. Shit, Sid asked Noble if he could come too. Noble said yes. I'm surprised Kelle's ass didn't ask. Noble chartered a private plane for us to fly here too. Child, you should have seen that pilot. He was hot!"

"Auntie, I'm so happy you are here."

"Me too. I'm glad we can meet these people together. You see your other sisters."

I look over and see Twaab sitting at a table with MJ and Jon. I start waving when I am tapped on my shoulder.

"Hello Virgie! I am Mrs. Winston! Is it alright if I give you a hug?"

"Yes ma'am. It is my pleasure to make your acquaintance." This lady looks better than Noble described. She is gorgeous! I mean drop dead gorgeous. She has brown hair with highlights. Her hair is styled with big, beautiful curls draping down her back. Mrs. Winston is wearing a silk two-piece pant suit.

"My baby! Give your mother a hug," she lets me go and holds her arms open to embrace Noble.

"Hello mother! I missed you! You look beautiful. Is that a new blouse?"

"I'm sure it is. They always dress me in new clothes when we have guests."

"Well, you look beautiful. They have great taste."

"Knucklehead don't act like you don't see me," a lady who is the spitting image of his mother says from behind Mrs. Winston.

"Kristin, I couldn't see you because you are so short. It's hard to look down from up here," as he makes a gesture with his hand towards the sky.

"Babe, this is my little sister Kristin. I mean little too. Kristin, this is my Virgie." She reaches out her hand and touches mine.

"Hello Virgie, my brother is so rude. How was your trip?"

"Hello, it was great," Noble gives me the side eye treatment. What else am I to say? I'm just meeting these people. I can't tell them all my business right at this moment.

"Virg, you were trying to fly all around the world without me. I guess we are not the sisters I thought we were."

"Natasha Janine! I hate you. I love you! No, I really hate you. No, I really love you! This is the happiest time of my life. Girl, none of this could happen without you telling all my damn secrets."

"Well, how else was he going to know? It had to be perfect. Tabitha and I made it happen."

"Noble, did you invite Tabitha?"

"Yes, I did! She is probably around here somewhere with Daryl I'm sure of it. Daryl visits here often."

"Wow, everyone is here! Thank you so much. I can't say it enough. Thank you!"

Kristin walks over and grabs her fiancé's arm but he's facing a table of people. I think she is going to bring him over here. Natasha Janine grabs my arm and drags me back to the entrance way.

"Virg, I need to warn you before you meet your future brother-in-law."

"Why? I don't know him."

"Yes, you do!"

"What?"

"It's Professor John Michael's son Lyon!"

"Our law professor?"

"Yes!"

"You have to be shitting me."

"I am not! We have already had our awkward moments."

"Are you serious? You cannot be serious. Lyon? Professor Michael's son? Let me see," as she leads me to the patio door and points to where he is.

It is surely him. Lyon Michael, my professor's gay son is marrying Noble's sister. Wow!

Lyon is cool. He supposedly genuinely loves Kristin. He also supposedly is very attentive to her and her needs. Shit, this is what any woman needs in a relationship. When we were in college. He was on the wild side. We thought it was because of his dad.

Professor Michael was a handful. His views on life were so rigid and one sided. Lyon is much younger than us. We would see him at parties, school events, and out with his friends. He would dress provocatively. He wore all black. He would sometimes dress in women's clothing and shoes. When we attended his family's dinner parties, he would make a scene by arguing with his dad. One time he smashed their dining room table because his mother asked him to use a coaster. He was out there. I'm wondering if I should say something or wait until he does. Let me walk out there before Noble thinks something is wrong.

"Babe I was wondering where you went. Everything okay?"

"You know how Natasha Janine and I are when we get together."

"My sister wants to introduce you to her fiancé. He says he knows you all from college. He is a little younger than you."

"Really?" I'm not saying shit.

"Virgie, I would like to introduce you to my fiancé Lyon Michael."

"Hey Virgie, it's been a while. Congratulations to you and Noble. How are you?

"Lyon, wow! Oh my God! When I last saw you," I was interrupted by him.

"Yeah, I know. A rebellious teenager pretending to be gay to piss my dad off." He wasn't gay, wow! Well, he is a great actor.

I'm in my thoughts when I hear Noble say, "What do you mean pretending to be gay. Kristin, you know about this." Lord, I'm not ready.

"Noble, congratulations man!" Jon says interjecting. He is holding my sister MJ's hand. She looks beautiful. It's amazing how a matter of weekends can change your whole life. I reach out to hug her and she says, "Sister, this man loves you just like we do."

She knows how to make me cry. He does. I want to love him back.

We are standing here talking when we hear someone talking behind us. "How the hell do you send all these people to my house? You didn't check shit out with me." This must be his uncle Connor." He looks like the actor from the movie. Shit, I can't recall the name.

Norman says, "This isn't your house. This is my damn brother's house!"

"Norman, this never was your brother's house. I told Noble when he told me your ass was coming that you probably won't leave here alive. Raq, you better not say a damn thing." This is a relief. They are just like us. Just like us, ghetto as hell.

"Uncle Connor, I see you are well and ready for the fight. This is my Virgie. Virgie, this is my uncle Connor."

"Hello uncle Connor. Thank you for welcoming my family into your home."

"Virgie, this isn't his home."

"Norman, leave Connor alone. Don't be a damn fool in front of our guests. You all are embarrassing Noble. Noble, tell them to stop it." As his mother says, walking towards Connor.

Noble says, "this is our home. Welcome to our home "The Winston Place."

Kristin says, "My brother told y'all in so many words to shut the hell up! That's why I love him." That's why I love him too.

# Sunday

Pinch me until I scream. This trip has been everything to me. I am still in awe. Noble took care of the details better than I would have. I never would have thought about doing something like this. I would have just booked us a flight and hotel. I wouldn't have thought of securing us transportation. Uber makes travel to and from so easy. You don't need to rent cars and download maps anymore.

My thoughts about traveling out of town were always surrounding Natasha Janine and I on some epic adventure. It would be us doing something wild and crazy. I remember when Natasha Janine and I went to Rome. We had our minds made up about having a one-night stand with an Italian man. We would walk or drive around Rome looking to find men we would like to make it happen with. We had so much fun. We were heading home by the time we thought about what we should have done or didn't do.

My note of love with Noble will be forever. I will hold on to it whenever I need to remember this moment. I know there will be times when he will get on my last nerve in our marriage. I will need to grab hold of this thought from my memory to push my way through. And I know there will be times when I will get on his nerves too. It is my hope that he grabs hold of a thought in his memory reminding him of why he loves me. Look at me over here thinking about our life in marriage. I will be a married woman. I like how it sounds.

"Babe, I love you!"

"I love you too Noble. Thank you for making sure my family is here to share in our engagement announcement. I'm so busy enjoying our time together I haven't shared anything."

"Well since the cat is out of the bag. I asked your sister MJ if she was okay with me marrying you."

"When?"

"Her and I went to lunch last week. It was after I told you about Laverne. You didn't leave me and that's when I knew. I didn't want you to ever leave."

"So, what did MJ say?"

"MJ told me that if I was serious, I needed to get everyone on board for this. She said that it wasn't an individual decision. She called all of them. And, I had to ask them one by one."

"Are you serious?"

"Yes, I am. The only person who gave me a hard time," as I interjected.

"Auntie?"

"No, it was Twaab. She told me that she thought I was gay."

I burst out laughing. "She actually said that to you, wow!"

"No, she said, "Are you gay?"

"I told her no then she said, I need you to be sure you are not because my sister is the real deal. And if you are trying to prove you are not by marrying her, then I need for you to move the fuck on."

"Wow! I didn't even know she cared that much."

"Babe, they love you immensely. Natasha Janine said if I was going to propose then it must be special. So, I rented the house. I was going to propose there. But I felt like you deserved so much more."

"Oh Noble, you gave more than I ever expected. This is the best proposal I've ever received. It's the only but still…"

"Babe, my mother is very sick. I know she looks and behaves like she is fine but she's not. I have only one great big ask of you."

"What is it?"

"I have invited everyone here for a wedding not an engagement announcement."

"A wedding? We just got engaged!"

"That's my big ask. Will you marry me tomorrow?"

"What? Are you serious? How? Do they know? Noble, tell me you are not serious."

"Babe, I promised my mother if I were to ever get married, I would do it on her birthday. Tomorrow is her birthday! And before she leaves this earth, I want her to be alert and happy. We will experience it together while she still can remember. When I asked your family for your hand, I made it clear what I wanted."

"Noble, this will be my marriage forever. I want to be a part of every aspect of it."

"Babe, you said you would trust me with the details. I have shown you that I can handle them with the detailed specifications. This is my big ask of you. If this wedding does not meet your criteria. I promise to marry you when, where, and how you want."

"Noble, this "ask" is bigger than I could imagine. I don't know. I have so many ideas of what my wedding will be, who would attend, where it will happen, and even who I would marry?"

"Who was it you were going to marry?"

"It's none of your business now. You have messed that up."

"Oh, I did huh? Well, I'm sure he could not match what I have done so far? And if you think he can, then tell him I am up for the challenge," as he kisses me in my mouth. He is always trying to distract me with his sexual advances. He is happy I'm down for the distractions. I will need to talk to my family first before I agree. But it will have to wait until I release this unexpected tension.

"You'll never play fair. You are kissing me knowing I can't make intellectual decisions when I am so aroused."

"Get used to it! There is no fairness with my love. I'm giving it to you every way I know how."

The things this man does to my body. Oh my! Sometimes I amaze myself. I am so open to anything he wants to do. At first, I was reluctant to even engage

114

in it. I can't think of the last time I had sex in a man's parents' house. I tried my best to whisper and squeal softly like he loves. But baby some of those twists and turns I couldn't hold back. It was funny how he quickly covered my mouth talking about his sister next door. It didn't stop him. He continued to give me all he had. This man bent me up like a pretzel. The way he held my legs in the air so I can feel all of him. He is lucky I didn't have him arrested. He was killing me in a good way. I need to take a nap this early in the morning.  Just so, I can get some of my energy back.

I have never slept in such a soft comfortable bed like this in my life. I need to pinch myself to make sure I'm not dreaming. I am sleeping in Noble's childhood bed with him. I am at his parents' house with our families and our best friends. What would make this even more perfect? I wish my mother and grandmother were here.

Can I really marry this man tomorrow? I wanted so desperately to have a long engagement. I wanted to say to so many people "my fiancée," strongly pronouncing the "cé" sound. Noble is asking me to give up on that dream for the sake of his mother's health. I can't even say that I am ready. We have literally been engaged since Thursday technically. Now I will have to tell people we had a short engagement.

"Babe, I knocked you out huh! Say it! Noble, daddy you knocked me!"

"Whatever!"

"No, you will not steal my moment. I want you to say it or we will have to start over again." No, the hell we are not.

"Noble, sweet dad-dy! You put it on me. Oh, you did that daddy! You spanked me, banged me, and squeezed me!"

"Stop it! I am getting aroused all over again. It's something about the way you are saying that." Now he is sucking my breasts.

"So, I guess you don't want me to answer your question."

"Okay I will stop. But the next time just say it, like I asked. You are starting fires then putting it out too fast for me to recover."

"Okay Daddy!"

"See, you're starting it again." We are laughing. I don't care how I say it. He will always be aroused.

I know I am a ball of emotions. I don't know how I will explain this to my family. I will need to talk to them outside of Noble's presence. I decided to take my family to a restaurant so we can talk freely. My Auntie is so mad we must walk. There was no one available to drive us to the gate. It feels like the house is a mile away. I'm surprised Dominica hasn't said anything since she has every right to complain. But she hasn't said a word. I ordered a vehicle to accommodate us. Auntie insisted that Mr. Sid come with us talking about "I'm not leaving my man behind when I leave, he must leave too." She is acting like Ms. Erlynn wants Mr. Sid.

116

"Virgie, I don't trust anybody with my man."

"Okay Auntie! He can come."

Noble referred us to this seafood restaurant on the riverwalk. He reserved a private room. He's still trying to show me he can handle the details. A beautiful young woman greeted us as we entered, she told us that we can order whatever we want. Apparently Noble told them to bill him. She states that she has strict instructions about not taking money from anyone in this party.

"Child, I had no plans of giving you any in the first place," says my Auntie. I see MJ giving me the look like "we already knew that." I quickly turn my head, so she doesn't see me laughing.

"Dominica, can you eat seafood?"

"MJ, you know I hate seafood. And I understand this isn't about what I want to eat. I will find something on the menu."

Mr. Sid is asking to speak with the chef. They are doing too much. I should have stayed at The Winston place.

Auntie is telling the waitress that she needs a glass for her dentures. Twaab is laughing. Natasha Janine acts like she is high. I don't know how I am going to ask their asses anything.

Brunch is delicious. We are having a great time now. I was quite nervous after the way they were acting when we arrived. Everyone is laughing, talking and cracking jokes. I hate to disturb all the fun we are having but I must.

"Family, I am so happy to share this moment in my life with each one of you. I asked that this time be about us. Noble dropped a big "ask" in my life. I want my answer to be reflective of our love."

"Virgie, we know what the big "ask" is. But it is a decision only you can make."

"MJ, you are right but I'm full of mixed emotions."

"Ms. Virgie, I have to say I don't know what you all are talking about."

"Mr. Sid, Noble wants us to get married tomorrow."

"Oh, hell no! Why does he need to marry you so soon?"

"Sid shut your ass up! You are only here because I asked if you could come. To be perfectly honest, I just wanted to fuck in a mansion instead of the senior assistant building. Hell, you could have stayed there until I got back if I knew that fine ass pilot would be with us."

"Kat, I let you say anything and everything, but this is her life. She shouldn't be rushed into making a lifetime commitment."

"Sister, I say marry the man. You love him and it's obvious he loves you."

"Dominica, crazy ass is making a point. And if I'm saying it then you know it is a damn good point. I don't agree with shit she says."

"I swear I can't stand my Auntie. My mother told me to watch your ass. I understand why."

"Dominica, watch your mouth! There will be no disrespect to Auntie whether you agree with her or not." Twaab is getting serious with her.

"Dominica, Twaab is right. Auntie is who she is, but you will not disrespect her." I need to support Twaab on this. Dominica will not start something so foul as this.

"MJ, you should say something. You see they are ganging up on me. Who is going to take up for me?" Dominica is acting like a child. She is out of line.

"If I can say something," as all my sisters and Auntie say in unison. "No, you may not," to Natasha Janine.

"Hold up. She can have a say! She's my best friend. Y'all will not treat her like she isn't. Natasha Janine, you can say what you want."

"Virgie, I'm so glad you are getting married."

"Y'all asses get on my last damn nerve with this shit. Let the damn girl talk. I'm sure she doesn't have anything else to add. Talk!"

"Thanks Auntie!" Auntie is rolling her eyes too hard. I don't know why she does this to Natasha Janine.

"Virg, I just wanted to say. Noble spoke to us all about this. He had reservations about how you would feel. We have all shared our perspectives about this. But the one thing I'm sure of is, he loves you more than life itself. And I know, you feel the same way about him. Marry the man you want to marry but do it only if it's your heart's desire. You have my blessings not because you need them. You have them because I would not want you to experience this moment without them."

"Wow, this damn girl did have something to say." Auntie knows how to mess something up. We all are laughing and crying.

"Ms. Virgie, I have a question for you."

"Okay Mr. Sid."

"Do you still have feelings for Kelle? Because if you do, I think you should resolve those first."

"Mr. Sid, that boat sailed a long time ago." MJ gave me the eye as if she knew my answer. I haven't thought about Kelle, but this is a good question.

"Sister, I say this. It's not about how you feel about Kelle. It's about how you feel about Noble. There will be people who will forever have a place in your heart. I must admit Kelle is that person. But does the love you have for Noble transcend that feeling. If that is the case, then marry Noble when and wherever he wants. You owe yourself a shot at this love, the way he loves you, and how hard he loves you."

"Thank you Twaab. You said that beautifully."

"And let me say this, I'm wearing what the hell I want to wear so miss me in the pastels."

I walk over to her to give her a great big hug when everyone walks behind me to form a larger hug. I love these people. And this is proof they love me too.

"Sister, I want to talk to you."

"MJ, what's wrong?"

"I just want to talk to you in private."

"Ok let's step over here. What's up?"

"Sister, I'm in love with Jon. I have never felt this way about anyone. I can't sleep. I can't eat. All I want is to spend the night laying in his arms."

"Awe, this is so sweet."

"He has been so patient with me. He hasn't pressured me for more. I can tell he wants it. I see what you and Noble have. I want that kind of love."

"MJ, I understand. I would say talk to Jon. What Noble and I do is right for us. You must do what is right for you all."

"Well, last night I did."

"Did what?" Oh Lord, I'm sorry for being such a negative influence on my sister. She has given herself to a man. It's totally my fault. Please don't punish her for this because of me. Allow her to have another chance. I will do what it takes to get her back on track.

"I slept the night in his arms. He told me that he loves me."

"Oh my God. What did you say?"

"I didn't say a word."

"Why not?"

"I haven't dated in years. Everything I know about it is before the social media era. We have only been dating for about two weeks."

"But you said you love him."

"I do but should I tell him."

Sunday

"What did Twaab say?" She tells her everything.

"I haven't told her yet. She knows I slept in his room. I don't know if I will right now."

"MJ, you need to tell him how you feel. Process your feelings together so there are no mixed messages. But I have to ask. Were you all clothed?"

"Yes! Why are you asking?"

"Because when a man sees you naked or half naked, they always tend to be in love."

"Sister, you are crazy! But he was rubbing my ass when he said it."

"See, I knew there was more to this story." I'm so happy for her. She deserves it. I know the reason why she doesn't want to tell Twaab. She thinks Twaab would see her just like us. And she wants to stay sanctimonious in Twaab's eyes. MJ does have an apple bottom shaped ass. Now that is probably what helped him discover his love for her.

We are pulling up to the gate and to my surprise Noble and Norman are waiting for us.

Noble is sitting in the cart with such a beautiful smile on his face. I'm wondering why they needed two carts instead of one.

"Babe, I'm here to pick you up. Uncle Norman will take everyone else back to the house."

"Aww, that's so sweet. Thanks baby!" Why is he giving me this wet kiss? What else does he have up his sleeve?

"I see you missed me."

122

"I did! I wanted to take you for a ride figuratively and literally. But first, we need to talk to my mother."

"What? Your mother? Why?"

"She asked to speak with us when you return."

I'm not ready for this. We are going to talk to his mother. I'm too grown for this. This can't be happening to me.

"Are you okay? I'm sure she just wants to get to know the woman I'm marrying."

"Are you sure? If she has dementia, she doesn't even know it's me she'll be talking with."

"Well, we will find out shortly." This right here may be too much to handle.

We walked into the house. It appears his mother is in her bedroom. Her bedroom expands across the house. It is the size of a one-bedroom suite. She has a parlor, a walk-in closet the size of a bedroom, a huge bathroom with a separate shower area and jacuzzi tub, and a balcony. It is on the second level of the home. Mrs. Erlynn is sitting on the balcony looking out over the garden.

Noble calls out to her, "Mother, I'm back! I brought someone for you to meet." She returns towards his voice and says, "It took you long enough."

"Hello Mrs. Winston! I am Virgie Mae Kelly."

"Hello Ms. Kelly! Please excuse my attire. I was resting. I decided to sit on the balcony. You, young people, please come and join me." She doesn't even remember meeting me yesterday. Her memory is quickly leaving her. I look over at Noble' face. I can see the hurt in his eyes. He clenches my hand a little tighter as we walk to the balcony. This must be so hard. You love a woman who your mother may never get to know. Now, I'm crying.

"Babe, everything is fine. You don't need to cry. I'm good, trust me."

"Okay, I will get it together."

"Noble, have you eaten yet? How about you Ms. Kelly? Or would you like to be called by your first name?"

"Mother, it's late afternoon. We both have eaten. Have you eaten yet?"

"I think I did. Kristin was just up here with her fiancé. His name escapes me. He did seem to be a nice young man."

"Well, I have not had the pleasure of talking with him yet."

"Mrs. Winston, you may call me Virgie."

"Okay Ms. Virgie. Are you a friend of Noble and Laverne?"

"Mother, this is my fiancée. You met her yesterday."

"Please forgive me. My memory comes and goes. I remember your face. How are you?"

"I'm doing great. You have a lovely home here."

"Thank you! It's the prison my husband built to keep me here locked up and isolated."

"Mother do not start with that. You can leave this place anytime you want. I can sell it tomorrow if you would like."

"Noble, it's true! However, I have become quite fond of this place. Virgie, I hope my statement didn't upset you. My husband decided that he needed to build a large house. He thought it was a good idea. He didn't want me to have a need to leave. His goal was to keep me here away from his other life. But I'm sure my son didn't share that." Noble is uncomfortable with her sharing this information. It's written all over his face.

"Mrs. Winston, I love this beautiful dress you have on. You look simply stunning."

"Virgie, you know Nigel killed himself." What the fuck? Oh my God! Noble didn't share that. This is fucked up.

"Mother, stop it or we are leaving. My father didn't kill himself. He died from cancer. Just stop it."

"I'm so sorry my memory keeps escaping me." She winks at me, giving me the Duchenne smile Noble is known for.

"Virgie, tell me about yourself. But first things first, why do you love my Noble?"

"I love Noble because he loves me. He loves me in ways I have never imagined to be loved. He stands with me ready to catch me when I fall. He holds me close, never letting me go. I love Noble! And tomorrow on your birthday, I will become his wife."

"What? You all are getting married on my birthdate. Noble was this the surprise you had for me. I can't believe it. There will be two weddings on the same date. My son and my daughter are both getting married. I would have never imagined being able to experience this kind of love shared amongst us all." What the fuck? She must be delirious. This lady has lost her damn mind. Two weddings on the same date. What the fuck have I agreed to? Speed wedding edition for the Winston's, oh hell no!

Noble has not said a word since we left his mother's room. He must know I am not in favor of something so ridiculous. Two weddings, two receptions, two of everything on the same day. Who would even agree to something so ludicrous? I need him to start talking because if I open my mouth first this will not be good.

"Sister, what's wrong? Jon and I were going to go for a walk. Do you and Noble want to go with us?"

"MJ, I think that would be a great idea. Where is Jon? I need to talk to him." Now he has something to say. He wants to go on this walk to avoid the conversation we need to have.

"Noble and I would love to go but we need to discuss some things."

"Babe, we are good. They are our guests. We should accompany them."

"Virgie, you all will be married soon. There will always be a time for discussion to take place." I see exactly what he is doing. Well, I am a firm believer in wherever you are is wherever you will get it. He has chosen the place. I will deliver.

We are walking along the garden. MJ and Jon look great together. She changed her clothes wearing a beautiful sundress. Jon is fine as hell. I love how confident he is holding her hand. They are such a cute couple. Noble's ass has his head down like he has lost his best friend. He knows he is wrong for this but still hasn't said shit about it.

"Noble, are you okay?" I know damn well he isn't.

"Yeah babe, I'm fine."

"What's going on with you two? There will be a wedding tomorrow. Why are you all so melancholy?"

"I think it's probably because everybody is getting married tomorrow." I'm telling everything. This shit isn't my secret to keep.

"Sister, what do you mean? Who else is getting married?"

"Noble, tell them. You are standing up here like you don't know. Tell your best friend and my sister who all are getting married tomorrow."

"Babe, let's not do this here."

"Do what? Tell my sister that her sister is getting married on the same day your sister is getting married. I think my family should know."

"What? Are you serious Virgie? Noble, this isn't what you discussed with us."

"Bro, I told you to tell her. Why didn't you tell her?" Oh, hell no! Jon knew about this. Noble knew about this. He knew and didn't tell me or my family. This is fucked up on all levels.

"You knew? This was planned. You misled me into believing this is about your love for me. And, how you want to share it with your mother. You are a liar!"

"Babe, it's not what you think. It's not."

"Sister, let him explain. There must be a logical answer for this. Noble, if you love her like you say you do then start talking. And start talking now."

"MJ, fuck what he has to say! I can't marry a man who can't," as Noble grabs my hands and puts them to his face.

"You can't marry a man who loves you. Is this what you are about to say? Because that's just it! I love you! Why does it always have to be more with you? My love for you isn't enough. I don't give a damn if I must attend hundreds of weddings with you before we are married. I have shown you countless times what you mean to me. But now, I ask what I mean to you. What do I mean to you? The man you love and respect. My mother is ill. This morning she asked my sister to get married on her birthday. Kristin is fully aware I asked you to do the same. So, without revealing that we may be possibly doing it, she agreed. You left this morning to discuss it with your family. It was never disclosed to me that you had agreed to my "ask" until you told my mother. Virgie, maybe you are right. You can't marry a man like me because of the image of the man you have in your head. And that is not me. I am not a liar. I have been completely honest with you. Maybe my therapist was right about you.

You are not ready for the man I am. It may be because of all the shit you are holding on to. Don't ever call me a liar."

"Noble!"

"Don't Noble me. You can and you have often said some hurtful shit. I am not a liar. And Babe, you will never call me that again." He storms away with Jon following behind him. MJ and I are just standing here.

"Sister, are you okay? What is happening? Talk to me. I feel like something is going on here. Let me help you, please!"

"MJ, I don't know what's wrong with me." Now I can't stop crying. What have I done? What is wrong with me?

"Sister, let it all out. You can't keep holding it in. Let it all out. It is going to be okay. I promise you it will be okay." This is the last thing I remember about us standing in that garden.

Everyone is on the patio. They are all smiling, laughing and having a great time. Noble is with Raq and Jon talking and smoking cigars. I'm sitting at the edge of the pool by myself. I'm just not in the mood. I know I really messed up. For the first time, I don't know what to say or do to change it.

I didn't see Mr. Sid. I glance up and he is standing directly over me.

"Hey Mr. Sid, are you okay?"

"That's my question to you. Are you okay? I see you sitting here like something is wrong. Is there something wrong?" I shouldn't say anything to him about what happened, but I need to talk to someone.

"Yeah, there is something wrong. I love Noble. But I am so afraid to do it. I know it sounds weird."

"It doesn't at all. Loving someone is complicated. Television makes it look easy but there is nothing easy about it."

"I'm learning the hard way. Kelle was easy to love because there were no expectations for me to meet. He just wanted someone by his side."

"But Mr. Noble is the same way. Ms. Virgie, I think what is holding you back is you. I am a watcher. I watch people and study their behavior. Kelle is my son and there is nothing I wouldn't do for him. But he will never make for a good husband. You have a man who will be a good husband. But it will not mean a thing if you don't think so too."

"I know Noble is a great husband."

"Then Ms. Virgie, it's you. Are you a good wife?"

"I don't know if I am."

"I talked to your aunt. She as well as your other family members. They don't believe you would be." Wow, they are over there having a great time on my man's dime. Why didn't they say something to me? Am I that woman? The woman who people are afraid to tell the truth. Do I give that energy off to others? The energy that sends people in the opposite direction. I'm even more confused now.

"Ms. Virgie, can I give you a piece of advice?"

"Sure!"

"Whether anyone else thinks you will make a good wife, ask yourself this. Does Mr. Noble think I would? He is the only person who signed up to spend the rest of his life with you. So instead of wallowing on your shortcomings, seek the thing that makes him look past them. You need to begin to see yourself as you want him to see you. Now that I have said my peace. Kelle sends his well wishes. I know it doesn't matter. I told him I would share it with you."

"Thank you, Mr. Sid."

"No thank you Ms. Virgie for being honest."

I still feel bad. It was great talking to Mr. Sid. But I don't know what's wrong with me. Why am I out to sabotage everything that may be good for me? I act as if I need to preserve something else for later. I need to get it together. The crazy part is I have less than 24 hours to do it. Noble seems to be in a good mood. Why can't they recognize my discontentment? Why can't they help me, help me? I wish I had the answers to my questions.

"Virgie, may I speak with you?"

"Sure Kristin!"

"I haven't had the chance to speak with you. I want to thank you for what you have done in my brother's life."

"I'm not sure if I understand."

"When Laverne died my brother was hopeless. He owned her death as if he killed her himself. He shut everyone out. I saw him often in despair. She was his everything but only because she wouldn't have it any other way. He loved her. I couldn't stand her or her twin sister." Wow, I'm at a loss for words.

"Virgie, she was the master manipulator. And my brother couldn't see it. It was her idea to put perimeters on how my brother cared for me. Noble isn't that guy. He is loving and giving. She put it in his head that I was reckless and naive. I'm smarter than she could ever imagine. I know you know about my fiancé's past life. He told me." She is blowing me away with this tea she is spilling.

"I love him beyond anything he has done in his past. I don't see life without him. He loves me and wants to spend the rest of his life with me. That's enough. My past isn't squeaky clean. He knows it too. My mother told me that she felt like you had a problem with the idea of two weddings on the same day. We are not prepared to wed tomorrow. I told her that to cover for Noble. He wanted so desperately to wed the woman of his dreams on our mother's birthdate. It's not my idea at all. But I haven't witnessed my mother this blissfully happy ever. If you would allow for us to join in your ceremony just for ceremonial purposes, it would mean the world to her. We wouldn't be getting married, but my mother would think we did. This is a "big" ask. If I can offer a suggestion, when I get married for real you can take part in my ceremony too." She is too sweet. Now we both are laughing and crying.

"Kristin, I would be honored to have you all a part of our ceremony. This conversation blessed me beyond what you could have imagined. I do love your brother. The fact you are sitting here sharing your love for your fiancé is the revelation I needed. Thank you so much. Tomorrow we will be two married women," as I start winking my eyes at her. "It will be our little secret."

"Thank you, Virgie. I'm so happy my brother found you. I am not only getting one sister but I'm getting four and a bonus one."

"A bonus?"

"Yes, Natasha Janine! I take it she is like a sister right."

"You are definitely right."

"But don't tell anyone, Dominica is my favorite. She is so funny. She can't remember anything."

"I get it totally. She is mine too. Don't tell them I said it either."

Noble walks up to us and says, "Babe, I want to go and lay down. Are you coming?"

"Yes Noble!" I'm glad he didn't go without me. I love him so much. We are walking to the room like nothing happened. He is rubbing my hand so softly. This man does it for me every time.

"I'm going to take a shower."

"Noble, can I join you?"

"Babe, I would love for you to but give me a minute." He isn't over it. Wow, he is rejecting me. This is so sad.

"Noble, I'm so sorry!"

"Babe, I'm not asking or expecting you to give me an apology. I want to take a shower and lay down. I want you to be here with me. This is all I can handle right now."

Is he crying? It looks like he is crying. He is crying.

"Noble, come here!" But I'm waiting for him to come. I am on my way to him.

"Noble, I love you! I love you! I hope you can understand that. My love for you makes me unsure of me, not you. I know who and what kind of man you are. This is new for me."

"What's new for you?"

"It is new for me to allow you to handle the functions of my life. I have cared for everyone. You desire to care for me. That's new. It's my own insecurities questioning you. The one question I am confident in the answer you will give is you love me. There is no doubt in my mind about it. Noble loves Virgie. Virgie loves Noble. So will you marry me on your mother's birth date after your sister gets married?"

"My sister isn't getting married."

"Yes, she is. We just talked about it."

"I will tell her she will not be getting married tomorrow. If there will be a wedding, there will only be one."

"Why are you saying if? Have you changed your mind? Is our wedding off? What's happening?"

"Babe, you must decide what it is you really want. Will the man I am, be enough? Enough for you to be happy. Enough for you to live happily ever after. So, if there is a wedding tomorrow you have to make the ultimate decision. I'm going to take that shower now."

I don't like the way he is talking to me. He is talking to me like I am not Virgie, the woman he loves. This is not good for either of us. I don't have a clue how to make this right. If I just go along with the wedding, I don't think it will be enough. I hope it will. He was so excited before. I can't explain why he is in this mood. Or even what is this mood. I'm going to wait until he comes out of the shower and give him some space. I need some space myself. Every time I think I have hit my recovery point someone says something. I'm reminded how fucked up I am. I know I don't hear a knock at the door. Really, someone is knocking.

"Excuse me Virgie. Is Noble in here?"

"Yeah Raq! He is in the shower."

"Can you tell him that Connor wants him to come to the parlor immediately?"

"Okay I will. Is there something wrong?"

"Yeah, my dad and Connor are going to kill each other. Noble is the only person who can get them right."

"Raq, move your ass out of the doorway. Ms. Thang, I need to speak with my nephew now. Where is he?"

"He is in the shower." Connor pushed past Raq heading towards the shower. He is banging on the door saying, "Noble bring your ass out of there. You brought this damn fool to my home. You better come get this mother fucker. Bring your ass out here."

Noble walks out of the bathroom with a bath towel wrapped around him. Oh my, he looks damn good with water still dripping off his body. Just looking at him is making these nipples rock hard.

"Child, close your damn mouth. You are in here acting like he isn't yours already." I couldn't help but burst out laughing at his uncle Connor.

"Uncle Connor, what's wrong? Can it please wait until I put some clothes on?"

"You know what the hell is wrong? Norman's walking around here like this is his house. You better get him before I get his ass."

"Connor, chill out with the threats."

"Raq, shut your trifling ass up. You lucky I even allow your trifling ass back in here after the shit you pulled." I'm not surprised by it. Raq is trifling as hell. I would love to know what it is. I see who I need to make my friend in this family.

"I will say this and this only. Leave my room now. I will be out there to handle it. You all can now go to your respective areas of this house." Damn, my man commands respect. They are all scared of Noble. Connor is the first to leave out. Raq is still in here talking about his father.

"Man, I hope you know what you are doing. These two together are ticking time bombs ready to go off simultaneously."

"I just wanted my family to witness the biggest moment of my life. Give me a minute, I will be out soon."

"I got you. I will keep them cool. I'm sorry about disturbing you, Virgie. This is our family as fucked up as it may seem." Raq hugs Noble before he leaves.

"Noble, are you good?"

"No, I'm not!"

"Is there something I can do?"

"Yes, come here." This is a serious moment and all he wants to do is fuck.

"Babe, I need you to believe me when I say I love you. I mean for real. Stop doubting that and feel my heart as it pours out onto you." Before I can say a word. There is silence. Wow, he is crying so hard. I want to say something. I better not. Now my tears are flowing too. We are standing in the middle of the room crying, now that's love.

"Babe, I need to take a nap before I deal with them. I will need my strength."

"Can I say something before you do that?"

"If it has anything to do with today, I rather you not. I want to rest peacefully. I want to feel your cushion on my leg. That's it."

"I just want to say. When you walked out here in that towel, my whole body yearned to release."

"Now that's worth talking about. I wanted you to shower with me but if you must ask after you said yes. I will always say no! I want you to always know you can share my shower, my heart, my love, and in my happiness."

"I noticed you didn't say your money."
"Enough of this talking before I really fall asleep without you releasing. I need you to hold me." He is standing here with his dick in his hand.

"It's my pleasure," as I pull and squeeze it.

Noble says, "You can have all my money if you keep holding me like this."

"Well, it's mine. I don't plan on changing that at all."

He is so bad, but I wouldn't have him any other way.

I feel like we were fucking for hours. Damn, it's only been 45 minutes. This is the last time we may fuck tonight. He fucked me like it was our last time as single people. He bent my legs over my head. I felt all of him. This isn't the first time I felt all of him, but it was different. He committed to every thrust, smack, suck, pull, and push he gave me. If this is the makeup sex, I may need to figure out how to argue more. Here I go with this fucked up thinking. I need to change my paradigm.

We are all sitting at the dinner table. I don't know what Noble said to Connor and Norman? They are playing quite nicely. My Auntie is a whole character. Her and Mr. Sid are telling everyone about how his blue pill works for hours. He acts as if he is really my uncle and she's, his wife.

Dominica and Kristin have a whole vibe. Twaab is laughing with Connor. Maybe what Noble needed was a release. It feels as if everyone has calmed down. We are doing great connecting as a family. I don't like the way Raq, and Natasha Janine are conversing. She is flirting with him. And to my surprise, he is receptive.

"Babe, are you okay? You appear to be preoccupied."

"Why is Natasha Janine over there with Raq? After everything that happened with those hoes. She should never talk to him again."

"So, I guess she hasn't told you?"

"Haven't you told me what?"

"She flew here with Raq."

"What? What the hell are you talking about?"

"Just what I said. You heard me clearly. They are good with each other."

"Oh, the hell they are not. I'm going over there to break that shit up. She has lost her damn mind. Oh, hell no! What? No! You can't be serious."

"You are going to do no such thing. I need everyone to be just like they are. You have a decision to make. This will be the first time, I'm sure of it. You tend to everyone other than yourself." No, this is not sitting well with me. Natasha Janine has picked a side. It's Raq's side too. Wow!

Sunday

Here we are back in the room. Noble is on the phone. He is talking with the catering company about the arrangements. He is so protective of the details for our wedding. I don't even have a clue about my wedding dress. I am going to need him to share something with me. I have had enough with this secrecy stuff he is doing.

"Hello! Hey MJ, what's up? Okay I will be downstairs in a few minutes." MJ is calling me. I wonder what is going on.

"Noble, I'm going downstairs with MJ. Do you need my input on anything before I leave?"

"No Babe! Please don't be down there long. I would like to make love to Ms. Virgie Mae Kelly before I'm married."

"Oh really! I think you have made love to her enough times already. You should start focusing on how you will make love to your wife so save your energy."

"Babe, stop playing. I have enough energy for them both." He is a whole mess.

As I am walking downstairs, I should stop by Natasha Janine and talk to her. I need to hear what she has to say about this. Now she is sleeping with the enemy. Hell no! You know what, I'm not going to say shit. She should have said something to me.

"Virgie, where are you going?" Damn, she just startled me.

"Mrs. Winston, I'm going to meet my sister downstairs."

"Can I come with you? I would love to meet your family."

She is losing her mind. She was talking to MJ all evening.

"Okay, we can go together." I hope MJ doesn't need to confide something in me.

"MJ, Mrs. Winston asked to join us if it's okay."

"It is! I am having all the ladies come so we have a little bachelorette fun before tomorrow."

"What? Did you all plan this?"

"Yes, we did! We would not let you get married without having a little fun."

"Noble wants me to come back to the room. He wants to have some fun too." I say as I giggle a little. He is going to think I did this on purpose since I said he should wait until we are married.

"Virgie, he knows what we are doing. He said you asked him to handle the details. This is one of them. The party is by the pool. And by the way, Noble already left with the fellas so I'm sure you will be fine." This man, the one I love, really took care of everything.

I can't believe how hard I laughed. We played games, talked shit, and ate our faces off. I can't believe all the gifts I received. Uncle Connor was the host of my party. He didn't want to go with Noble because Norman went with them. I'm happy he stayed with me. I don't think I would have had fun without him. He walked out of the house to the pool with a basket of boas. He danced around placing one on each of us.

Mrs. Winston had a whole vibe. I could see Auntie getting jealous of the attention she was getting. I had to tell Auntie that nothing would change between us. I don't know why I felt I had to do it. I am glad I did. Auntie immediately started to relax and join in the festivities. Kristin and Dominica are best friends forever. They were inseparable. Dominica even told me that she wanted to move to Atlanta with her. I told her to pump her brakes. But if I know her like I do, she will try to do it. I need to tell Twaab and MJ.

Natasha Janine didn't say a word about Raq. I know she knows I know. Especially since I was giving her the side eye the whole party. She just laughed and stayed over by Twaab with this goofy look on her face. I don't understand why she is keeping secrets from me. She will always leave me to go get some dick. I already know her ass. I'm sure they are fucking again. She did not fly all the way here on some "friend" shit. I know her too well.

Noble interrupts my thought. "Babe, did you have a good time?"

"I did. I am having the time of my life. Your family and my family party well together. Your uncle Connor is a mess."

"He is definitely that, but he will be your uncle in a matter of hours."

"Wow, I'm getting married. I don't know what I'm wearing, the color, who is giving me away, who my bridesmaids are, the order of our program, the music that will be played, or nothing. This feels so

142

weird to me. I feel like I landed on an island without any indication what I am supposed to do."

"Babe, we are getting married tomorrow. I don't care if we do it in the nude, the only thing that matters to me is you as the bride and I am the groom. Furthermore, there are four dresses in the closet, please choose one or all for our ceremony. I picked one in your favorite color, a traditional gown, your dream gown from what I am told. I also picked a sexy one too. The sexy one is my choice. I already have decided on enough details for you."

"What? Are you serious? How? Who helped you with this?"

"Your family was very instrumental in this. We have a group text, and everyone added input. Natasha Janine did all the shopping. She has had your back this whole process. She even made sure the gowns met the price you want to spend. I could never pull this off without her. It is my prayer that you one day share every one of your desires with me like you have shared with her. I want to be the one who knows it all."

"This is so sweet. I have only talked to Natasha Janine without judgment in my life. I would love to share everything with you. I know I will not. The beauty of knowing everything about me is knowing you will know where to find it out. I want us to have friends and have lives separate from each other."

"But when it comes to your desires, I am the only person who needs to know. I need you to promise me that. I will be the only person."

"You will be the only person who will know. I promise! I love you!"

"I hope you know I love you more each time I think of you. You are my babe forever."

Now, we will make love until it's time to walk down the aisle. He knew I wasn't going to just let his comment stand. It must be coupled with actions. But before I could initiate, he beat me to it. This man, my Noble who loves me. He has snatched this dress right off me. Wow!

"Baby, do you need me?"

"Why are you asking me that?"

"Because you are ready. I wanted to take charge this last time before we are married. I promise you will forever be able to lead, take charge, and care for me but give me this one."

"Babe, I will always do as you will have me."

"Now lay back and enjoy this adventure."

# Monday

I cannot believe I will be a married woman in six hours. I should have held back all that sex so I would have some energy left. I rode Noble all morning. I laid him back on the bed and pulled his pants off. I was surprised that he went out with the fella's commando style because he always wears briefs. When I asked him about it, he said he showered when he returned and threw some pants on to come get me. To be honest the thought of him with the fellas like that turned me on. It is probably what made me go as hard as I did. After I pulled his pants off, I started stroking him with my hands. I was a maniac.

I used my mouth first to get him wet so my hands could do the rest. I watched him just "ooo" and "ahh" while he scurried in the bed. I began massaging his thighs. He told me to stop but I couldn't. I needed to control this moment of passion. I was determined to return the favor. He bit me on the thighs, so I bit him. Noble yelled out but that didn't stop me. He yelled so loud Jon knocked on the door to check if everything was okay. He told him we were good, and I continued. I moved up his thighs and started sucking his dick again. I was tenacious. I ran my teeth across the top to inflict a little pain and continued to suck vigorously. When I thought he was about to cum, I took it out of my mouth and used my hand to finish the job. I stared in his face the whole time. I just knew it felt good to him by his smile. And then, I got on top of him and straddled him with my ass facing him. It was the first time in months my knees did not give out on me. I rode him to finish him again. But I needed to straddle him from the front. I wanted him to see my breasts bounce up and down. I knew Noble wasn't going to let me be the one to finish our soliloquy. He sat up and flipped me over. It was all him until he wiped himself out. Now, I am lying here looking at him sleeping like a baby. I can't even feel my toes.

"Virg, you are getting married. I thought I would get married before you. You always run away when things get serious. Wow! I am in total disbelief."

"Natasha Janine, I don't know how you thought you would get married before me. Your ass doesn't even know if you are gay or straight."

"I do know. I am straight! But I like to have a good time."

"Girl, shut the hell up. Whatever!"

"I do know Virgie. And you know what else I know. I like Raq a lot too!"

"What! This man almost destroyed you and your career. As soon as this wedding is over, I'm taking your ass to the psyche hospital. You have lost your damn mind."

"Virgie, It's complicated. I'm not crazy! I like him! I always have!"

"What? Natasha Janine, You're crazy!"

"Virgie, this isn't the time or place to discuss it. It's your wedding day. Let's finish getting you ready to walk down the aisle to you forever."

"I'm making time. I will not be standing up there thinking about this shit. You can tell me now. Give me the clip notes version."

"When you first introduced me to him, I was instantly attracted to him. He is so charismatic and fine. He has everything I like in a man. He is tall, dark, rich, and has a big dick he knows how to use."

"Save those details. I can't stand his trifling ass. I need you to speed this up."

"Well, I did what he asked because of how I was feeling towards him. I know the things he does are fucked up to, but I never stopped liking him. To be honest I probably started messing around with Mari in hopes it would keep me with him. That's why I'm saying it's complicated. We talked every day last week. We talked about everything that happened. Raq apologized repeatedly. He asked if I wanted to come here with him to help with the final arrangements, so I did. We are in a good space. We have laugh, cried, and even fucked. I like him. And I want you to give us a chance."

"Are you serious?" I don't know what else to say. She can't be serious.

"I am serious. We are leaving tonight to go to Toronto for a couple of days."

"I can't believe you. Are you serious?"

"I really am. I want you to ease up on him. What happened between him, and I was on us. I need you to allow me to make my mistakes. I will always have you in my corner for whatever life throws at me and the same for me with you. Raq is who I chose. You have the right to be happy or disapprove of my choice. But Virgie it still is my choice. I hope you will be happy. I love you! I don't want to keep what makes me happy from you anymore."

"Wow! I'm speechless but I love you too. I have made some bad choices myself and you stuck with me. I don't really know if he is a good or bad choice. I do know you are right. It's your choice. If you are happy then I'm happy. Now can we finish getting me ready. I'm about to get married!"

My best friend is finding her own happy place. I'm happy for her but not her choice. I don't see him changing and that's the part that pulls at me.

She is caught up in her feelings which is clouding her judgment. Natasha Janine isn't being the smart attorney I know. So how can she be so naive about this dude? Raq is fucked up. Uncle Connor even said so. I'll talk to Noble about this after the honeymoon. I'm not letting this shit fuck up our moment. Honeymoon? Are we leaving immediately for a honeymoon? I hope our trip to Italy wasn't it. If it is, that would suck. No! My Noble has something planned, I'm sure of it.

"Virgie Mae, I want to talk to you."

"Sure Auntie! Thank you for being here with me."

"I wouldn't miss this for the world even if I had to pay for it myself. You know how I hate spending my own money."

"Yes, I do!" She doesn't have a problem spending mine though.

"You are about to make a big decision about your life. I want to know that you are sure about this. Sid said he talked to you. He doesn't think, you are sure. Are you sure about this?"

"This is the easiest decision I have ever made. I want to spend the rest of my life with Noble. I wasn't sure if I wanted to do it today."

"Well, you get to make that decision baby. What is the rush? Are you knocked up? Because Noble said it's about his mother. There isn't shit wrong with her ass. I see how she looks at Sid. That bitch has all her facilities." This lady and her protectiveness for her man.

"She is quite well. Noble wanted us to get married here with her while she is well. She is diagnosed with dementia. There is only a matter of time until her memory will fade. He wants her to be a part of his wedding now.

"Wow, that's beautiful. Well, I'm glad you told me because I was going to check her ass. I don't give a damn that this is her house. Child, you saved me. I will make Sid dance with her. This way she will have a memory of a beautiful black man with a salt and pepper beard making her all hot and bothered."

"Auntie, you are a mess!"

"I know if my memory starts to fade away, take my ass to a strip club. I want to have a memory of a big black dick stroking me up and down. That's the only memory I will need. Shit, I don't want to remember half of the shit I have already seen."

Why does it feel like forever before I walk down the aisle? Noble told me that he wanted our wedding to be about us. There are no bridesmaids or groomsmen. It will solely be us. He promised that if I decide to have another wedding where I can manage all the details he will comply. I think I might but who knows. This wedding, maybe, is all I need. All I need for a new start to change the way I am thinking of myself. The way I feel about the things I desire and my Noble. He is the person I want to share it with.

"Sister, you look stunning!"

"Aww, thanks Twaab! You look quite dapper yourself. I'm glad you decided to wear that tuxedo skirt suit."

"MJ made me wear it."

"No, I did not. You wore it because you like it. Tell the truth."

"She is right. I wore it because I like it."

"What about me? How do I look?"

"Dominica, I don't know anyone who could have pulled off a floral black and white dress like you."

"Really? Y'all aren't shit."

"No little sister, you look good."

"Thanks, Twaab. I know you mean it too." Everyone just burst out laughing.

That's how we do when we get together. We are serious, playful, and silly.

"As the oldest, I thought that we should say goodbye to the single Virgie."

"Wow, that hoe is leaving the building. MJ, you are ready to get rid of her already."

"Virgie, be serious. I want us to pray together we are touching and agreeing with you about your forever."

"Okay, you know how silly I am when I'm nervous."

Twaab reaches out and hugs me saying, "Sister you have a great man who loves you. The reason I know is because he shows it. He loves you out loud for the world to see. Instead of being nervous about his love, be excited for it. It will bring a level of happiness you haven't experienced."

"With that being said. Let us pray! Lord looks over my sister Virgie. May she embark upon the beauty of love. May it be multiplied to produce great accomplishments for her and Noble's union. May she follow the lead of her husband. May she trust the direction he takes their family. May they be blessed with children to nurture and provide for. May they work whatever their differences are, out with each other. Lord, help them keep you as the head of their lives in Jesus's name."

"Thank you, MJ, for that prayer. Twaab, you will always be my voice of reason. Dominica, there is nothing in this world I would not do for you. You all are my sisters. And I thank God that you assisted my fiancé with the details of my marriage."

"Are you going to tell them, or am I?"

"Dominica tells them what?"

"Virgie tells them?" I look over at Dominica. I am reminded of exactly what she is talking about.

"Tell them sister."

"Dominica, how do you know? It never crossed my mind."

"What never crossed your mind?"

"MJ, she is talking about how I haven't had a period in over a month!"

"What? Are you serious?"

"Twaab, yes, I am. Dominica, how did you know?"

"Because ever since I started to have a period. Our periods are always together. Last night, it hit me. You haven't had one because you haven't called me once to complain about it."

"I may be pregnant. This cannot be true."

"Twaab, ask Jon to take you to the store for a kit. Go now! We can find out before you get married."

"Wait a minute. We are moving too fast. Let me think about this for a minute first."

"Virgie, you need to know now. Let Twaab go get a kit. Trust me!"

"Okay MJ!"

"Virgie, no crying. We will have time to cry later. Please!"

I walk into the bathroom and close the door. This couldn't be happening to me. I am about to get married to the man of my dreams. And I may be

152

pregnant too. Wow! How the fuck did I miss this? How the fuck didn't I protect myself?

What will Noble say? Will he still want to marry me? Will he think I trapped him? Will he want a baby? We have never talked about children. He knows Dominica is pregnant but me too. What will he think?

"Who is it?"

"Me Virg. Let me in!"

"Natasha Janine, give me a moment. I want to be by myself for a minute."

"We are in this together. Open this door and open it now." Let me open this door or she will continue to knock.

"Virg, what's going on? I just left you. MJ called me to come back because I may need to refresh your makeup. Why?"

"Dominica pointed out that I haven't had a period."

"You didn't know you didn't have a period? How would Dominica know that? I didn't even know that shit. I pride myself on knowing everything about your ass."

"She knows because we have had the same menstrual cycle since she started hers. Every month like clockwork we will call each other to either say it's coming, it's here, or complain about our cramps."

"Are you serious? I never knew this."

"Yes I am. MJ sent Twaab to get a pregnancy kit with Jon."

"Have you told Noble?"

"It's only been minutes since I had this revelation so no, I haven't told him."

"This is beautiful!"

"What's so beautiful about being pregnant on your wedding day?"

"It just is."

We are all sitting in my room. Auntie, MJ, Twaab, Natasha Janine, and Kristin are in here. Dominica's ass invited her talking about how she will be your sister soon. I don't even know her. I want to cuss Dominica's bad news ass out. She always must tell some shit. She is like the third eye. She sees all. Twaab was back within minutes with the kit. I couldn't even piss on it by myself. All their asses were standing in the bathroom watching me. I can't believe this. This is some wild shit.

"I will read the results by myself. Everyone can return to the garden. I don't want Noble to be nervous. I will share my results with you all. I will need to be left alone just to process all of this."

"She's right. Let's leave her alone."

"Thanks MJ!"

I am walking down the aisle to wed my Noble. He looks so handsome. I should pinch myself to confirm this is real. I'm walking to the melody of my favorite song. My family should be excited. I am about to make a lifetime commitment to the man I love. But they are all looking nervous. They are curious about the results. I wish they wouldn't look so obvious. They are dead giveaways to the fact something is going on. I look over and see Mr. Sid smiling from ear to ear. This means Auntie hasn't shared with him yet. Connor looks good. He is a sharp dresser. Norman is sitting next to Raq and Natasha. I can't believe I'm saying that to myself. Natasha Janine and Raq are a couple. Wow! This is really it. My last walk as a single, independent, and self-sufficient woman. The last stroll on my road alone.

I am standing here about to marry the man of my dreams. But is this fair to Noble? I haven't even looked at the results from the pregnancy test. I placed the stick inside my bra. It was taking forever to reveal whether I have a pink or blue line. If I didn't come out when I did, Noble would worry about me. Maybe I should've waited. How can I stand here and lawfully wed him? He never talked about having a child. We don't even know each other. I can only imagine what he would think if there's a pink line affirming, I am pregnant. I should say something or at least do something. I'm more confused now more than ever.

"Will Noble Winston take Virgie Mae Kelly to be your lawfully wedded wife?"

"I will!"

I can hear the preacher say, "Will Virgie Mae Kelly take Noble Winston to be your lawfully wedded husband?" I am drowning in the silence of the room. Can they hear me say yes? I want to desperately say yes. But my mouth will not let my lips move.

And I can hear him say it again, "Will Virgie Mae Kelly take Noble Winston to be your lawfully wedded husband?"

Noble leans in and whispers, "Babe what's wrong?"

# Epilogue

This week had us all on the edge of our seats. Virgie and Noble are about to make a life changing decision. Why does Virgie make it so hard to love her? We heard what she has to say but is there more. Noble wants to love her forever but she acts like that is not enough. Noble has finally made the introductions with Virgie and his family.

# About the Author

S. S. Suggs knows firsthand what sensual encounters can do for romantic relationships. The author is well sought after for relationship advice and ideas for exchanges of intimacy. S. S. Suggs is a graduate with a bachelor's degree in Sociology (the study of human behavior) and a master's degree in Arts and Science.

S. S. Suggs is a storyteller who enjoys exploring the imagery of sensual encounters, bringing sensual encounters to life through her words. As expressed in the book series beginning with volume one, the readers became captivated by the story of Virgie and Noble as they journeyed together daily loving each other differently. It was not until volume two, the readers were able to learn more about who these characters are and the mystery behind their relationship. It is with a background in human behavior and arts and sciences, the author uses her education to help people through the complexity of relationships. With a love for details and descriptive language, the author takes an approach on word play to audiences from all backgrounds.

www.ingramcontent.com/pod-product-compliance
Lightning Source LLC
Chambersburg PA
CBHW060417260626
47161CB00013B/1732